Deadman Humour

Thirteen Fears of a Clown

Deadman Humour

Thirteen Fears of a Clown

Edited by
Dave Higgins

And featuring stories by
R.M. Mizia
Henry Snider
Steven Pirie
Donna J.W. Munro
Christopher Stanley
N.D. Coley
Roger Jackson
Christopher Degni
Lee Glenwright
Samantha Bryant
Charles R. Bernard
Joshua R. Smith
G.K. Lomax

First published September 2019.

ISBN: 978-1-912674-06-0

Cover Image: ©2019 Henry Snider

Published by Abstruse Press, Bristol (http://davehigginspublishing.co.uk)

Contents

Introduction

While Stephen King's Pennywise is almost certainly the most famous clown-monster today, my first encounter with the idea of inhuman creatures that looked like clowns was *Killer Clowns from Outer Space*. Of course, as with many people, my first encounter with apparently inhuman clowns who turned out not to be was Scooby Doo.

And all of that would have remained a set of cultural references I shared with British geeks born around the same time I was if Misha Burnett (whose work appears in the companion volume to this one) hadn't challenged authors he knew to publish at least one anthology this year.

Along with the serious challenge, he shared a humorous genre generator to "help" anyone who needed inspiration for a theme. Like a literary version of a giant sideshow roulette, my attempt landed on "horror noir clowns on the run".

At first, it was merely a passing chuckle. However, it reminded my unconscious of all those clowns who weren't, all those times it had seemed like clowns were monsters.

So, I flipped it around: what if the clowns were running from a supernatural horror? What if the clowns were the ones pulling the disguise off the monster to reveal the truth?

I'd intended to release a single anthology with a mix of supernatural and mundane threats. However, I received many more great submissions than I needed. So, I've compiled two anthologies: this one, filled with stories where the fantastical is real; and a companion volume where the darkness is entirely human.

These thirteen tales are about clowns who aren't the real bad guy: clowns fighting the unspeakable; clowns accepting the true power of their profession; clowns discovering not all magic is sleight-of-hand.

These are the fears of a clown.

—Dave Higgins, 22nd July 2019

The Living Dark

R.M. Mizia

It wasn't entirely odd to hold a birthday party at night. Not really. Some parents Charles had met were actually pretty anal about that kind of stuff—what time the party was, that is.

My little so and so was born at ten-thirty p.m., the parents would defend in an as-a-matter-of-fact tone. *If it's a BIRTHDAY party, then it needs to be as authentic as possible. Just like New Year's. You celebrate it at twelve o'clock in the morning because that's when it happens.*

Righty-O then. And that was fine with Charles, because either way, he would get paid for the two hours he performed. Plus, he wasn't much of a morning person, and preferred his lunchtimes—when many parties and engagements typically took place—open and free.

He enjoyed being a clown for children at birthday parties. The hours were more than lax; the payment was decent—not compared to a hundred thousand dollar a year salary, no, but compared to a teacher's earnings, it was a nice chunk of change; he could choose which events to take and which events to decline; he was his own boss.

Really, there were no draw backs.

OK, there were a few... But in all actuality they were fairly inconsequential.

There was the occasional beef with the stage magicians—who felt as though clowns were outdated and less than comical, particularly Charles.

They were just jealous though.

Charles had learned quite a few slight-of-hand tricks himself to add to his routine, just so he could diversify his client base. And all in all, he was rather good—better than Trickso, the self-proclaimed master of birthday party magic tricks. A clown that was also a class act magician? A-OK! Two for the price of one!

There was the growing less frequent—but still common—angry parent, who felt as though their precious little angel had been duped of a real show. Some threw temper tantrums about how their kid was less than amused with Charles' acts—when in reality, it was more like their wallets had been less than satisfied.

Charles always made sure to give a complete list of his acts to the parents upon his booking—particularly so they would know what they were purchasing, and so there would be no surprises later on. There were many horror stories within the birthday party community of hired acts—always clowns for some reason—showing up wasted off their ass and throwing up in the hydrangeas.

Charles was a professional, and wanted his potential clients to know that.

Oh yes! This will be perfect! the parents would say with enthusiasm. *Little so and so and their friends will absolutely LOVE this!*

And for the most part, that was true. Charles was always able to pull a respectable amount of admiration from the children he performed before. Oohs would course through the air when he made a laser light jump from one hand to the other. Aahs would come when he turned two dozen balloons into a massive water hippo. Amused laughter would belt out when he would trick some of the kids into smelling the Black Eyed Suzan on his shirt collar—at which time would squirt out water. And there was always a more than hearty round of applause at the end of his act—especially at the end of night parties, where the use of phosphorescent glow powders brought along even more astonishment.

Charles figured the disapproval from the parents came from some subconscious source. Perhaps they had loved clowns as children themselves, and now that they were older, they could see just how silly clowns actually were. How *childish* they were. Perhaps they were hoping to find the same amount of astonishment from their youth.

But Charles knew that was false hope. Clowns weren't for adults. Not really.

And even though he could rouse up a healthy level of excitement from the kids at parties, there were always a few who were deathly afraid of him. For whatever reason—somewhat unbeknownst to Charles—there *always* were.

His costume was rather un-scary, he thought. Charles tried to stay away from the big, rainbow colored afros and floppy shoes. No bedraggled, dirty, hobo clowns, no sad clowns, no face paint that would make him look menacing in any way, shape, or form. Only happy smiles and eyes, bright colors, and no acting overly happy like many clowns do—that was scary enough on its own, even for a normal person. He was a clown after all, not some deranged lunatic.

But even though he went through—what some in the clown business called *painstaking and unnecessary*—labors to keep kids from being afraid of him, there were always one or two who would bawl and scream their way through the performance.

5

He had been successful in the past of calming a few woeful children—showing them that clowns weren't bad at all—and eventually ended up performing at their own birthday parties, joyously welcomed with open and unafraid arms. But more often than not, these kids wanted nothing to do with him.

Nothing.

The gig was booked by a Mrs. Evylin Moore, a young, very well to do widow whose little girl was turning six.

This is a very important time in her life, the email had said, *especially since her father's passing. It's of the utmost importance that she be surrounded by love, laughter, and quality entertainment to keep her mind from wandering too dark. A task I hope a clown—and partial stage magician —will be able to accomplish. There is nothing more youthful than the antics of a clown.*

That was perfectly fine with Charles. And in fact, he couldn't have agreed more with the little quip about the youthfulness of clowns.

The parents at birthday parties were generally unconcerned with his performance—unless they thought it was too childish, that is. But every once in a while, a parent would get more than involved with his acts, sometimes even joining in on the fun. And that was fine, too. Because the adults would be chortling along just as much as the kids—assumedly something they hadn't done since their own youth by the looks of them.

My estate is large and there will be many guests—I hope you will be able to revitalize all of our lives as we need it very much. The party starts at eleven-thirty, so please be prompt. Tardiness will not be excused!

The address was close to the bottom of the email. Charles knew exactly where it was—in fact, only two miles down the road from where he lived. Though, to the best of his memory, he couldn't recall a particularly large home within the area.

That—coupled with the fact that Mrs. Evylin Moore hadn't listed an end time for the party—led Charles to believe this was a trick; one that had been pulled on him from time to time by shithead teenagers or belligerent stage magicians.

In the eight years that he'd been a children's birthday performer, he had had the shit beat out of him six times by baseball bat wielding, teenage assholes. Two of the six had sent him to the emergency room for punctured lungs and internal bleeding—both times, he looked like he had been run over by a car more than beat with a ball bat.

It took Charles a while to catch on—it was always the same kids and their email never changed—but eventually he learned how to tell the fake, ass-kicking for fun emails from the serious, we-want-your-business ones.

Charles sent an email back in response: *I'd be more than happy to perform at your daughter's birthday party. However, as you may or may not know, I only do two-hour performances. Sometimes I do less—at an obviously reduced rate—but I never go over two hours.*

A couple of hours later, Mrs. Evylin Moore responded with: *Yes, I am well aware of your operating times. Though I doubt we will actually need you for the full two hours—little Cynthia may bore of you quickly—I will be sure to give you the full fee, no matter how long we may actually require your services.*

Naturally, this was more than fine with Charles. His full two hour fee for maybe not even two hours work? He'd be stupid not to take the opportunity. And if his act did come to the full two hours? Not a big deal.

7

The Living Dark

Charles would look back on it as a day's work done—*Night, to be more precise,* he told himself.

———

The party was four days after Charles received the booking. He had had a steady stream of parties up till that point, and had been looking forward to it. One of his friends—a stage magician of all things—had convinced him he needed a vacation.

"You work yourself to death, man," his friend had said. "I'm starting to think that isn't dark paint around your eyes, and that its tiredness coming to the fore."

Charles agreed almost immediately. For some reason, the thought of taking a vacation had never occurred to him—perhaps because he enjoyed his job, and it wasn't very taxing or difficult, at least not at his age. But as soon as he heard the words *You need a vacation,* he whole heartedly agreed.

He figured a week would be good enough to recharge the old batteries. But as to where, he wasn't sure; that was something to be decided after the party.

———

Charles walked—not because he didn't have a car, but because it was a nice, warm, cloudless night. And still, after eight years of performing for little kids as a clown, he still wasn't exempt from the pre-party jitters every performer had. Some bit of nervousness that always told him something, *something,* might not go right. The walk allowed him to work it off, burn the excess energy away. Plus, the house was only two miles away; why not walk?

The road was dark and quiet. And since it was eleven o'clock at night, it seemed darker and quieter than ever before. Charles could hear creaks and moans and groans and snapping twigs off in the woods beyond the sides of the road. The owls and yearly Whippoorwills were quiet—along with the crickets and spring peepers.

But even though the air was still—Charles' shoes grinding and crunching along the asphalt being the only real noise—he could still tell the darkness wasn't empty. It was the extrasensory notion that something was watching him, following him, stalking him. It was the thing that raised the hair on the back of his neck when he was alone in a dark room—*knew* he was alone—but couldn't shake the notion of a set of eyes fixed upon him.

The living dark, his father used to call it.

The exact same feeling of unease he'd had every time before those shithead teenagers came out from behind a tree to beat the hell out of him. He was feeling worried now—*terrified* was more like it—that it would happen again. For the seventh time!

"Damn it," Charles muttered. "I knew I should have brought a flashlight."

There was a loud snap in the woods off to his left, like some large limb breaking.

Charles turned and stared into the darkness, straining his eyes and trying desperately to see what it was. But there was nothing. Or at least, *he* couldn't see anything.

"H-h-hello?" Charles said with a quivering voice. "W-w-who's out there?"

No answer.

And why would there be anyone out there? Charles quickly thought, trying to calm himself. *It's dark and spooky out here. I'm just hearing things and getting myself all worked up over nothing.*

He turned to start back down the road.

Another loud snap, this time, closer.

Charles twisted back around. "O-O-OK, wh-wh-whoever you are, you better just stop it now! I-I-I have a gun and I'm not afraid to use it!"

Not true in the slightest—why would a children's birthday party clown carry a gun? That's ludicrous. But whoever—or whatever, for that matter—was out there didn't know that. Charles knew that sometimes that act of brandishing a gun could deter an attack. So why couldn't the same be true for just *saying* he had a gun?

Best to stay away then, Charles thought. *Just in case. Better safe than sorry.*

There were no more snapping noises, but Charles' blood suddenly ran cold—he literally felt a chill flow through his veins.

He couldn't actually gauge the distance in the darkness—though, he knew it had to be close—but there was a pair of bright yellow eyes lingering within the black of the wood. They were solid—unblinking—and their gaze was solidly fixed on Charles.

They looked *human...*

Charles could feel his hands shaking and his knees beginning to quiver. His skin broke out into gooseflesh and he suddenly felt the urge to run—if he did that, though, his makeup would surely be ruined.

But that suddenly became a novelty, as more sets of bright yellow eyes began to appear next to the first set. His makeup could be corrected and brought back. His life couldn't be.

Charles' fight or flight instincts began to kick in, and naturally, he chose flight—his makeup could be fixed later.

I should have just drove, Charles thought.

But as he turned, a blinding wash of yellowish-white lights flooded past him. He raised his arms to shield his eyes, and once the light was gone, he lowered them—Charles saw the fading reds of a car's taillights, the groan of the exhaust filling the once silent night with pollution.

Charles felt himself calmer now—not by much, but it was enough for him to actually think things through now. He turned back to the woods.

The eyes were gone.

The house came up fast—he made an effort to hustle the rest of the way, just in case the yellow eyes came back.

It was a large, white thing that reminded Charles of some sprawling manor that would have been used as a slave plantation back in the 1800's. He knew the address—he had to drive past it just to get into town—but now understood why he had never seen the house before: the driveway was thickly wooded and zigzagged along for about half a mile, making it invisible to the main road.

Charles rang the doorbell, and though it took some time, a lady finally opened the door.

"Mister Wilmot, I presume?" the lady said.

Charles gave a courtesy nod. "Yes, ma'am. I'm Charles Wilmot. A pleasure to meet you." He extended his hand to shake.

The woman ignored it.

"Evylin Moore," she said flatly.

The woman looked both young and old—her skin was tight and supple looking, but there was more than a fair amount of wrinkles around her eyes and mouth. Charles thought perhaps the death of a close loved one did that to a person.

She was wearing a flowing, black dress with black pearls draped around her neck. Charles saw a couple of people walking past the door, and noticed that they too were wearing all black.

"Missus, I don't mean to sound rude or anything, but is this a six-year-old's birthday party or a funeral?"

Charles smiled to make it seem like what he had just said was a joke—which in reality, wasn't true—but all the same, it was his job to make jokes.

Mrs. Evylin Moore did not seem amused.

"Please, come in now, Mister Wilmot," she said in the same flat tone. "We have only a few more guests to arrive, and then the festivities can fully begin. Feel free to wander about and warm up the crowd."

Charles smiled brightly and gave another courtesy nod. Evylin Moore opened the front door all the way, and with that, Charles stepped in.

It certainly wasn't like any birthday party he had ever been to before. The atmosphere was dark and quiet and solemn—just like a funeral. The light was a dim, eggshell white that made Charles feel depressed—his outfit was probably the loudest thing in the house. There were flowers, but instead of the typical vibrant and lifefull flowers, they were grey and dead—Charles figured if he touched them, they would crumple to ash.

There was music, but instead of the custom *Happy Birthday*—or any of the standard birthday party tunes for that matter—it was sad violin and piano numbers. He had seen a lot of strange things throughout his eight years of clowning around, but this absolutely took the cake for strangest.

And the worst part? Charles wasn't even the only clown.

———

He had considered storming up to Mrs. Evylin Moore in a fit of anger, ready to tell her that he did parties alone. And if she didn't like that? Well, for all Charles cared, the young old coot could go fly a kite.

But Hank Dolan—a man Charles went to high school who also turned to be a birthday party clown—caught his eye.

"What the hell are you doing here, Hank?" Charles said in a harsh, quiet tone.

He hadn't seen any kids—which was odd—but that didn't mean they couldn't be around somewhere near where they could hear him.

"I could ask you just the same question, Charles."

"This is my gig, the lady emailed me a couple of days ago about it. Said she wanted a clown for her daughter's birthday party, but that I may not be needed for the whole time. Said I'd still get full payment."

Hank Dolan nodded in a slightly confused manner. "Same."

Charles gave his head a slight shake, as if here were trying to fight off an oncoming stupor.

"And I'm pretty sure that's how it stands for the rest of them, too."

Charles looked around the room. Sprinkled throughout the dark and depressing black wear of the party guests, were brightly clad clowns with an assortment of different styled hairs. Most were jumping about in front of people, laughing loudly, telling jokes— *Trying too hard*, Charles grouchily thought. And then there were others, who, just like Charles and Hank Dolan, were grouped up, talking amongst themselves, wondering just what exactly they had gotten themselves into.

"Have you seen any kids?" Charles asked Hank.

He shook his head, concerned. "Not a one."

"What's with this music? And the flowers? Did we get duped into working a funeral?"

Hank Shrugged. "Not sure. But there's no reason for there to be more than one clown at this party."

"And how did you figure that?" The sarcasm was heavy in Charles' voice, but Hank answered all the same.

"Just look around. There's what? Twenty-five? Thirty people here? The most I've ever had by myself was fifty, and everything was perfectly fine for me. I know you've had more."

True. Charles had once performed for over one-hundred and forty-seven kids—at an elementary school of course, but it was still a lot of people. There looked to be about nine clowns in total. He knew just as well as Hank that one clown—even a lousy one at that—could have served the party just fine.

Or whatever this is, Charles thought.

———

There were several doors within the ballroom where Charles and Hank and all the other guests had congregated. Each were open, and each were just as dark as it had been outside on Charles' walk over.

And just as on the walk, Charles had the feeling his father called *the living dark*. He couldn't see anything, but there was something, *something* just waiting beyond the doorways. Waiting for the right time to come out.

Once—on a round with Hank to see what good warming up the party guests would do—his heart nearly beat out of his chest.

The eyes...

The yellow, *human* eyes...

He had seen them—just one set—within the darkness beyond a doorway.

"Hey, Charles, you're looking rather pale. Are you alright?" Hank asked with an authentic worry.

But before Charles could actually answer, the heavy foot falls that were the clacking of Mrs. Evylin Moore's high heel shoes overtook the spacious ballroom, loudly echoing about.

"Ladies and gentlemen," she said with an enthused tone. "Our last few guests have finally arrived. I'm pleased to announce that the festivities that will revitalize us all, can now begin."

Three clowns...

There were three new clowns standing behind Mrs. Evylin Moore.

"Did she just call those three Wayne Gacys the last few guests?" Hank asked, leaning close to Charles.

"I think so."

Charles turned back to the dark doorway where the yellow eyes had been.

They were still there, staring at him—Charles felt as though he could hear something now as well. A low noise. Maybe a deep growling. Or perhaps it was a low chanting.

But that's what it was. Charles attention was broken from the yellow eyes within the darkness and he could actually hear it. The chanting.

Dachaun...

Dachaun...

Dachaun demoriey...

Three men came around and grabbed Charles and Hank by their arms. They were led to the center of the ballroom where the other clowns had also now been placed.

Dachaun...

Dachaun...

Dachaun demoriey...

All of the guests—men and women with young old faces like that of Mrs. Evylin Moore—circled around the clowns, their dark wear now more depressing than ever. Each of their mouths moved in sync, chanting along.

Dachaun...

Dachaun...

Dachaun demoriey...

Charles threw his gaze toward the open doors—their darkness was seeping out into the room now. There were more yellow eyes to accompany the first set, now slowly moving closer.

Dachaun...

Dachaun...

Dachaun demoriey...

The ballroom was growing dark—too dark for Charles to actually see anything other than the yellow eyes. Then a white-green light began to glow from the floor—a circle all of the clowns were standing in. There was strange writing on the outer edge of it. Charles hadn't noticed it before.

Dachaun...

Dachaun...

Dachaun demoriey...

The light from the floor illuminated all of the guest's faces, bathing them like the flame of a fire washes the darkness in a wood.

And now Charles could see what they were, the things with the yellow eyes.

They were not human. Charles didn't know what they were.

They were tall and dark, and their flesh now seemed to glow like a dying ember. They had horns and scales all over their bodies, and their teeth were horrible—like that of some ancient dinosaur.

16

Dachaun...

Dachaun...

Dachaun demoriey...

"Let me out!" shouted one of the other clowns. "Let me out now! I can't take it! It's driving me insane!"

The man began to rush the crowd of people encircling them all; before any of the other clowns could stop him, the man disappeared. Vwoosh! Vanished into thin air.

All that seemed to be left of him was a small pile of ashes on the ground. Charles felt his intestines crawl as he noticed the crowd around them now looked younger, more youthful than before.

"Why are you doing this?" Hank Dolan shouted furiously.

The circle of light—with the strange writing around the outer edge—began to shrink, scrunching all of the clowns tighter and tighter together. They all saw what happened to the other guy—the one who turned into ash—and didn't want to be the next victim.

"Because," Mrs. Evylin Moore said, "there is nothing more youthful than the antics of a clown."

The circle began closing fast now, the clowns huddled ever tighter and tighter, trying to keep it from touching them. But one by one—layer by layer —as the light touched them, each clown disappeared into a pile of dark ash upon the ballroom floor.

And the crowd of people encircling them grew younger and younger.

Dachaun...

Dachaun...

Dachaun demoriey...

Charles Wilmot had believed all his life that clowns got a bad rap.

Sure, some could be scary—even he found a few who creeped him out. But all and all, they were just normal people trying to make a living by cheering other people up. There was nothing wrong with that. It was pop culture and a few bad apples that made clowns so nefarious to the masses.

And before he fell to the pile of ash upon the floor in that ballroom, Charles was certain of one thing. More certain of it than he had ever been of anything else before in his life. It was that they—the clowns—had been the least scary thing in that room.

The lights in the ballroom came back to the same eggshell-white color as before and the music resumed playing. The creatures with the yellow eyes were now gone—presumably holed back up in their dark rooms.

Mrs. Evylin Moore stepped out from the crowd of people—now a visible fifteen years younger—and approached the pile of ashes. She knelt down once there and took a handful. She raised her hand and let all of it fall back to the ground.

"It was a good haul this month, friends," she said in a nostalgic tone. "Yarlond would be proud of us. All of you."

"Same time next month, Missus Moore?" said one of the women in the crowd.

"Of course."

R.M. Mizia lives in West Virginia and serves in the US Navy. This is his first published short story.

The Clown

Henry Snider

Smells of rancid popcorn permeated the air, leaving a buttery film on all that breathed. Lisa Welsley leaned forward, rested elbows to knees and studied each street performer along the boardwalk with detached scrutiny. Geeks walked past, each offered a different take on their iron stomach, the last of whom bit the end off of a bottle and pierced his cheek in the process. Blood strained through his grizzled beard as it changed color from dishwater blond to burnt amber.

"Thon-of-a-bith," the geek managed to the jovial laughter of those who succeeded where he failed. He dislodged the green glass and shook his head as a wet dog would, spraying bloody spittle across the wooden boardwalk and peppered Lisa's white sneakers.

"Asshole," she murmured.

Barkers shouted out insults and challenges to passersby, daring them to prove their worth at various games of chance. A wisp of cotton candy escaped its machine only to be carried away by the night breeze. Lisa watched it, momentarily transfixed by the pink fluff as it danced over the rail, lifting higher before it disappeared beyond the shine of the lights. Her eyes returned to the rather tasteless striptease performed outside of one tent that offered more patch than substance. She counted over half a dozen cracks and man-made holes along the side of the clapboard and canvas structure for those too cheap to pay for their extracurricular activities. An involuntary shiver coursed through her as one of the patrons stopped in the entrance, stared back at her and smiled a Cheshire cat grin before entering.

Then the clown appeared again.

Decked out in classic midget clown attire, no bigger than a meter tall, the entertainer wound its way through the crowd, oversized red plastic sunglasses bobbed with each exaggerated step. A couple, obviously on vacation, tried to get the small character's attention for a photograph but only succeeded in running into locals as the little black and white comedian darted between legs and navigated strollers with practiced ease. Lisa hopped down from the concrete fence and trotted after the green-haired performer.

The clown threaded its way to the strip club's entrance and looked back. It scanned the crowd and hunted for someone. Lisa ducked down, pulled the red ball cap low and continued to close in on the small form. As she closed in, the clown focused on her. It backed up the two risers, stepped behind the show's barker and peeked, to the catcalling amusement of all, from between the tall man's legs and waved a flyer emphatically at everyone.

"Shit," Lisa mumbled.

"Right here, right here!" The barker called out and tapped his cane against the clown's backside. "We have them short and tall, thick and thin, dry and...well...." He used the tip of the cane to lift the side of a dancer's robe and flashed a length of ghost-white hip where panties, if there were any, would have rested. She smacked the cane away in mock modesty and resumed her gyrating pre-show actions.

Lisa stood at the front of the crowd, a solitary Eve to a collection of eager Adams. She and the clown stared at each other from less than a handful of steps. The teen's hand went out, palm up, in the hopes to coax the small quarry down from its chosen perch.

Suddenly the clown pushed the barker from his stoop. The man staggered and waved the cane as he fought to regain balance. Lisa instinctively reached out, caught the man and tried her best to steady his skeletal form. He recovered, stood upright, then grabbed her by the hand and pulled the teen two steps onto the makeshift stage.

Shock and embarrassment flushed Lisa's face red. She stared at the clown who looked up from less than two feet away. White cake makeup covered exposed flesh where costume did not, though now smears showed hints of the brown skin below. Heavy forehead wrinkles marked where the semi-bald wig began. Cheeks sat sallow below the oversized shades and gave the impression of malnutrition to anyone who bothered to take more than a cursory glance. A sudden jerk on her jean jacket twisted Lisa to the barker.

"See here, one and all." He let go and she staggered down one step. "Even this pretty little doe wants to see Dante's Delights." The barker towered over Lisa, breath stinking of soured fish and chips. "You do want to see what we have to offer inside, don't you?" He stood upright just as quick and vertigo left Lisa dizzy. The clown squatted down, slid over the riser's corner and disappeared down the short alley where she saw so many beams of light escape the girlie show. The showman's silver bird's head cane handle lowered and pressed against her chest.

"Hey!" A smack at the cane but only succeeded in hooking it into her tee shirt's collar. Balance gone, Lisa performed her own stumbling act, similar in form to that of the barker's a moment before. The cane's beak ensnared both shirt and bra before it ripped free and freed the teen to land hard on the ground. Ocean air bit at the newly exposed skin and she scrambled to cover herself amidst the throng of onlookers.

"I...sorry...," the barker began before hearing the assembled crowd cheer and whoop at the sudden flash of nipple. What began a second before as concern hardened once more to a money-driven game face. "See that folks? Women can't even keep their clothes on just standing in front of my fine establishment." A volley of lewd suggestions flew from mouths, things so sick Lisa couldn't fully fathom. The showman continued and drew the crowd's attention back to the dancer he'd previously taunted. She took the opportunity to backpedal to the riser's edge and followed the clown into the alley.

Lisa took two steps into the alley and stopped. A few beams of light shot out at different angles and offered sparse illumination to navigate the narrow passage by. Bags and other bound refuse littered the ground. A stink no better than the barker's breath permeated the air.

At the far end of the alley stood the clown's silhouette, outlined perfectly against a gray night. It didn't move.

Lisa took the opportunity to pull a bobby pin from under her hat and threaded it through the torn portion of her shirt. She bent the metal over, anchoring the collar to the tattered front once more.

"There's no place to go." Her voice echoed louder than intended. "Just come on. Please?" A forced smile played across her face. "Come with me."

The clown's head cocked to one side, considered the dilemma, then shook side to side with an automated slowness and waved the flyer up and down as if it were a bird's wing.

"Heh. I'll go with you, sweetness."

Lisa looked down to the nearest bundle and recognized it now for a bum taking advantage of one of the holes in the dance hall wall. From the way he hunched as he looked over one shoulder, there was no question of the activity he currently engaged in.

Instinct screamed for Lisa to turn and run into the veritable safety of the boardwalk crowd...but that led away from the clown. She couldn't do that.

"Piss off!" She closed in on the clown in two self-assured steps.

The bum's hand shot out and grasped her around the calf, snaring the appendage to his position. "Aww. Don't be like that."

His hand felt hot, disgustingly warm and she thanked the stars above for choosing to wear jeans tonight instead of shorts despite the warm weather. Lisa kicked free and the bum tumbled. Rather than look back, she continued toward the shadowed form at the far end of the alley. The bum rustled to right himself as the distance between teen and clown grew short.

Ten feet.

Seven.

Lisa reached out again. "Don't be scared."

Five.

The clown took off with surprising speed, darted to the left and shimmied along the narrow space between the rear of a tent and the pier's rail. With no desire to lose what little distance gained by the last few minutes, Lisa squeezed behind the shop and followed her pint-sized leader.

"Heyyyyyyy...," the bum said from right behind her. "You don't wanna go that way. The railing's rotted. You best come with me."

A hand brushed against Lisa's ponytail. She scooted faster, then sprinted a handful of steps before daring a look back. The bum still stood at the alley's entrance, arm still outstretched toward her. All the lectures her mother gave about being safe and treating every solitary location as the ideal place for a rapist to take advantage surfaced. The man's hair, now visible, hung in sweaty clumps and offered no hint of shower's past.

The Clown

Her chest hurt.

At first Lisa attributed it to the cane head, but it really hadn't impacted hard. This was something else. Her breath hitched. Inhaling required a conscious effort. Lisa leaned on the rail to steady herself, felt the rotten wood lean, then crack and threaten to give way.

Panic. I'm having a panic attack.

The clown...her clown stopped at the end of the next tent. Its head gaze darted from side to side, unsure whether to continue along the backs of the structures, take the alley back out to the boardwalk proper or descend the barred ladder to the beach below.

Finally, a break. "Don't move. That ladder's dangerous."

The clown took a step towards the single metal bar that stopped access to the ladder, jerking movements appeared to be a little dance, daring her to speed up.

"I mean it." Lisa took two more steps. Behind her, the bum called out something, but whatever it was ended up stolen by the ocean breeze. Lisa reached out, grasped air as the clown shot underneath the metal bar and worked the rungs with practiced agility.

Lisa dove. Half her body slid under the bar and out into space before she reached down and grabbed the clown's black and white striped shoulder. A rung broke and the clown fell out into open air, a comical half cartwheel ensued as gravity laid claim to it.

"No!"

The figure shrank in size until she was sure it would disappear all-together. Lisa froze and felt no less than a half dozen splinters bite into her belly, each doing its own part to keep the teen on the pier.

Then the clown struck water.

A gray poof in an otherwise sea of black showed the impact.

She squinted and tried to make out the clown in the blackness.

Nothing...then lighter pinpricks moved in the dark. The clown fought against the ocean's pull and half swam itself under the boardwalk.

"Damn it," she breathed. "Not again"

After Lisa freed herself from the anchored splinters, she followed down the ladder, careful to test each rung before putting full weight on it. Repeated glances down offered little hope to pinpoint which way the clown went. Gray caps from waves that struck pillars reflected any light.

Ten minutes of careful decent brought her to the final rung. Still the distance to the waterline looked dangerous. The rung groaned...cracked, then sent the teen splashing into icy water.

Lisa bobbed gasping to the surface, only to have a wave steal the breath and knock her into the pillar she'd just climbed down.

She grabbed at the wooden beam and leaned against it while she fought for breath. Seawater fell from her mouth with each coughing exhale.

"No...more," she said around gasping heaves for breath.

Blades of parallel light streaked the sand and offered a soft illumination from the myriad of activities a few dozen feet above. Trash, netted by an ever-present length of seaweed blanketed an otherwise beige surface of sand. There, among all the other forgotten debris crawled the clown. It moved in slow motion, one hand reached out, pulled itself forward, then it stretched out the opposite hand to mimic the first.

Lisa pursued and kicked her way through the black water, Lisa pursued. She took a moment to study the small form.

Soaked fabric clung to the clown and showed a figure significantly smaller than the wire-assisted barrel waistline proclaimed. Oversized sunglasses, now dislodged, hung loose around the costume's collar.

Lisa kicked out and caught the clown in the hip. It jerked away.

"No...more," she repeated.

A second kick rolled the clown onto its back, revealing a handful of blonde locks that peeked out from the wig. Locks identical to Lisa's. Cake makeup washed away by the ocean, left leathery skin exposed. Shriveled sockets stared up at her from a face dead two years this past Halloween.

"Iiiiiiaaaahhhh...," the mouth worked, "...wuh...wuh...."

Lisa kicked out a third time and caught her little sister in the ribs and exploded a word from the child's corpse.

"Wuhon't," the child barked.

Another sneakered blow rolled the small corpse onto its side. "Won't what?" She kicked again and one toe painfully struck the child's pelvis. The impact rolled the clown onto her belly again. "Tell?" Lisa knelt. "Is that what you were going to say, Carrie? That you're not going to tell?"

Lisa stood and backed two steps. Adrenaline kicked in. "Of course you're going to tell, Carrie. You always tell."

Carrie reached brittle hands out and pulled herself another foot away from her big sister.

"You told about Ted and I in the shower." Lisa returned, rolled the clown-corpse onto her back and straddled her. "You told about me sneaking out." She smacked Carrie across the face. White makeup sloughed off along with some of the skin that held it in place. Slitted leathery skin, stretched drum-taught across empty sockets, stared up at the teen. "You told about my suspension." Another smack loosened the bald wig further, exposing a deep depression just above the left ear.

One of Carrie's arms raised to hold off the attack.

Lisa knocked it away.

"You tell, Carrie. That's what you do." Lisa emphasized each of the last four words by thunking a finger hollowly against the corpse's forehead.

"Iaaahhhhhhh," Carrie said.

Lisa adjusted her position and let both knees rest on the girl's chest. She felt the corpse struggle to inhale, just as it had every month for the last two years. Her knees dug in and a rib cracked. Carrie struggled harder, heels kicked into the sand and dug for purchase.

Hands reached up, grabbed at Lisa and fought to dislodge her.

"No more!" Lisa brought both hands down, smashing them into the clown's face. Bone buckled and the child's skull bloomed open to the night air.

Carrie's kicks stopped.

"No more," Lisa repeated, voice no more than a whisper. She sat with her little sister for a time and watched the waves smack against water-soaked pillars. An hour later found the teen covered in sand and standing atop a small rise on the beach. Blood ran fresh from the meat of her left hand, a train track pattern of teeth marks carved a vicious half moon into the palm. The scarred remains of similar wounds peppered up and down her arm.

The flyer, showing a cherubic little girl with lettering asking, "HAVE YOU SEEN ME?" blew free from the nearby seaweed and disappeared into the night.

"You won't tell this time, Carrie. I won't let you."

Henry Snider is a founding member of Fiction Foundry (est. 2012) and the award-winning Colorado Springs Fiction Writer's Group (1996-2013).

During the last two decades he's dedicated his time to helping others tighten their writing through critique groups, classes, lectures, prison prose programs, and high school fiction contests. Thirteen years to the month from founding the group, he retired from the CSFWG presidency in January, 2009. After a much needed vacation he returned to the literary world. While still reserving enough time to pursue his own fiction aspirations, he continues to be active in the writing community through classes, editing services, and advice. Henry lives in Colorado with his wife, fellow author and editor Hollie Snider, and numerous neurotic animals, including, of course, Fizzgig, the token black cat.

To Pull a Child from a Woman

Steven Pirie

"There, look, Whiteface." Hobo grins, though in truth he's not fond of having his hands smeared with blood. He"s not keen on crunching rabbit bones with hammer and pliers. This close to Whiteface, Hobo feels sweat gathering over his greasepaint. "I've made a new rabbit."

"Yes, yes," says Whiteface. "To pull a rabbit from a rabbit is *almost* a worthy trick."

"Almost, Whiteface?" Hobo steps nervously from oversized foot to oversized foot. He fights the urge to pull flags from his sleeve. He forces calm on his spinning bow tie.

"To pull a child from a woman and have the child live to tell of the tale, now that would be a trick worthy of a *real* clown."

Hobo frowns. He doesn't like it when Whiteface talks of *real* clowning. Hobo's caravan is littered with bits of rabbits, some of them still twitching and pulsing most pitifully. His carpet is sticky with blood. And the smell; such a fetid stench to an animal's opened insides that Hobo might retch.

"But what if I pull the child out dead, Whiteface? Or worse, only half formed? I'll be taken away and whipped, and thrown in jail and

29

left to rot. Jail is no place for a clown like me. They'll take my face paint away."

"Nevertheless," says Whiteface, "this is your task. You shall perform it under the top this very Saturday evening. Then we'll call you Harlequin, and you'll be Hobo no more."

"Saturday? Can such a trick be mastered by then?"

"By Saturday," says Whiteface, "or Hobo you'll always remain."

There are books, Hobo knows. All clowns, no matter how lowly, how pitiful, know of the great tomes of clown lore. Dust-brushed and web-worried, they lurk to the left of centre upon miles of shelving connected to every library in the land. They tug at clowns' dreams as they sleep.

Hobo hesitates at the stone-fronted library building. He doesn't like public places. They're full of folks who don't hide their faces behind a thick smearing of greasepaint. Their eyes and noses and mouths are naked to too many expressions. It makes it hard for Hobo to judge their mood.

Hobo quietens his heart, stops the blood gushing in his veins, pauses his spinning bow tie, and when all is still he can hear the books stirring within. He shivers; do they whisper words of welcome? Or do they laugh at him, cruel and harsh?

Hobo climbs the steps. It's cold inside the library. The librarian, a stereotype in thick-set glasses, bun-raised hair and locked away bosoms, stares as Hobo's oversized boots flap on her library floor.

"Children's parties," she says, coldly, "are held in the Town Hall next door."

Hobo pulls flags from his sleeve. He often does so when confronted by authority. He's not used to talking to women. He hops nervously from heel to heel. The little horn in each shoe parps apologetically. "I'm, um, here to see the books, Miss."

"The books?" The librarian's eye twitches. Care lines crease her forehead. "Please tell me you're after books on train spotting, or stamp collecting. Or this one just come in." She raises aloft the first book she fumbles upon the otherwise tidy counter. "Neo-Conservatism and Its Place in Modern Britain."

"I wish to see the books upon clown lore."

"Clown lore; are you sure?"

"I must learn a new trick."

The librarian wipes her brow with a delicate kerchief. Hobo looks away.

"Very well, come this way." The librarian glances at the trail of flags still pulling from Hobo's sleeve. "But for God's sake, no funny business. You'll have the books all frenzied."

Down steps, they go; stairs that go down but don't come back up; along a corridor which turns to the left, the left, the left, and to the left again but doesn't lead Hobo back to where he'd started. They cross great halls, striding on the ceiling, glancing down upon unsuspecting library goers lost in periodicals below. Once, in a particularly wide but narrow, winding but straight corridor, Hobo thinks he sees himself in the distance, but when he waves he doesn't wave back.

"I'm looking for a book that has a trick of pulling a child from a woman," says Hobo, as they walk. "Do you have one?"

"A difficult trick, I'm told," says the librarian. She rubs a hand across her stomach as she speaks. She looks pensive, though the expression is lost on Hobo. "So very difficult."

"Are you in pain, Miss?"

"I'm sure you'd not understand."

31

To Pull a Child from a Woman

Hobo *feels* a tear form in her eye. Sometimes it's easier to feel such things rather than look too closely. He stumbles, fearing it's him that's made her cry. Once, when he'd made the Bearded Painted Fat Lady cry, Mr Smoulder had threatened to shoot Hobo from his cannon.

"I hear that trick is fraught with dangers," says the librarian.

"I've to learn it by Saturday."

"Then I wish you luck."

They pause at a vault door. It's icy cold, chilled as if to subdue the books within. Brooding, that's what Hobo feels the books to be doing. The shelves go on for ever, an infinity of volumes lost in mists of time and space and beyond.

"Here. Clown lore," says the librarian. "Try not to get them throwing buckets of paper. Take control of their words. Make them think you're a Whiteface."

"But I'm only a Hobo."

The librarian touches Hobo's arm. Hobo flinches. Her palm is warm. The only woman ever to touch him was his mother, and then so brief, so fleeting a touch. Hobo feels his face flush.

"I'd not think like that," says the librarian. "The last Hobo who thought like that is still in there somewhere."

Even as he reads the spines, and the words tingle on his lips and form colours in his head, Hobo hears the books' taunts.

Hobo's got a girlfriend...

"I do not," says Hobo.

She touched his arm...

They're probably having babies now...

"That's plain silly," says Hobo.

I think he got a big one when she touched his arm...

Hobo's got a big one...

"Have not."

She can't have babies...

That's true, she keeps losing them...

Careless, that is...

Drops them out, drip by drip...

"She does?" Hobo pauses.

A bloody mess on the library floor...

Hobo's making a bloody mess...

Drip... drip... drip...

Hobo finds the book. *The Fine Art of Pulling Children from Women.* As he drags it from the shelf a second book falls fluttering open at his feet. For a moment he stares at it before reaching down and picking it up. It feels of greater power than the first. It feels older, wiser. Hobo grins and takes both books away.

Ah, the swirl of sawdust under the decorated ponies' hooves; the dance of spotlights off sequin-bedecked high wire maidens; the roar of mammoths as they rumble about the ring, each with a clown midget dangling by the braces from the tip of one of its great ivory tusks. Up near the top's roof, pterodactyls circle silently, effortlessly, watchful.

There's the blare of trumpets as the ring master, majestic in plumes of silver and green, steps out from behind the curtain at the top's rear: "My Lords, my Ladies and Gentlemen, welcome to the Circe Macabre. Pray be seated. Be seated and pray. For tonight, for your very dark delectations and perverse pleasures, I give you Mrs Elms and her Exploding Emus!"

Hobo shivers in the wings. It's not cold.

"Have you mastered the trick?" says Whiteface appearing over Hobo's shoulder.

"I've learned it, Clown-master."

"But not yet attempted it?"

"I've not found anyone willing to let me practice on them. None of the trapeze maidens want a child pulling from them. They called me Dullard, and Simpleton, Whiteface, and threw stones at me."

"Did you not ask the night-ladies at the docks? Or the homeless huddled in the doorways? Or the mad women in the asylum?"

Hobo shakes his head. Whiteface seems *whiter*, fiercer, as if that were possible. "It didn't seem right, Whiteface. I couldn't bring myself do it. I don't want to hurt anyone. I don't want to kill someone. Can I not do another trick? Can I burn Harlequin in ice-blue flames, or bury the Bearded Painted Fat Lady alive in flesh-eating worms? Can I shoot Mr Smoulder from the cannon?"

Hobo whimpers as Whiteface raises an arm as if to strike him. The clown-master glares down at him. His eyes are piercing green.

"You'll do the trick tonight, or I'll cast you out."

"But...'

"Cast you out for good."

————————

Alone, lost to dark thoughts while Mrs Elms' emus leap and snarl and *boom*, Hobo mumbles the trick's mantra over and over.

Take a woman young and bare, from her pubis find a single hair.

Hobo wonders back to the time he'd first found the circus. No, to when the circus had found him, orphaned, alone, clinging to life. How young he'd been, and how much he owed Whiteface in raising him. Like a father, Whiteface had been.

Lift it to the line of sight, blow it to a gentle flight...

Hobo brings his arm to his face. He can still smell the librarian's scent where she'd touched him. It's a delicate mix of Paris and soap and dusty books. He *breathes* her fears, *tastes* her sadness, aches at her losses.

Whiteface... a terrible, terrible father.

A gamete teased from fallopian gloom, pressed down into welcoming womb. Take one spermatozoa, rapid, vibrant, impatient...

Hobo thinks of his mother; how small and fragile she'd looked as Whiteface had stood over her; how the sawdust had billowed as she'd fought him; how she'd stained it red with her blood; how still and calm she'd looked, grinning with her guts spilled open, torn in birthing a fully grown child clown.

She'd gripped Hobo as she lay dying, as the wild horsemen had leapt into the ring and the circus went by, pulling him close into her. She smelled of Paris and greasepaint and intestines. "This is not your fault," she whispered. Five words, that's all they shared. A mother and son should share a lifetime more than that, shouldn't they? A son should not look down on his mother torn apart, should he?

Trumpets blare again. Beyond the curtains, Hobo watches as the carnies scoop up what's left of Mrs Elms' emus. The Harlequins are already out there clowning for the audience, riding miniature unicycles and throwing buckets of purple water, doing things with balloons and doves and squirting flowers. They've got ten mammoths balanced wobbling on each others' backs. Hobo feels Whiteface move behind him once more.

"It's time, Hobo."

Hobo nods. "Yes, master, it is."

Hobo steps out into the ring. The glare of the spotlights burn his eyes. Was he ever really meant for such a life? He spins his bow tie, and pulls flags from his sleeves, absently, distracted, because he knows for sure the librarian's here under the top. Even amongst the mammoth shit he can smell Paris and soap and dusty books. He feels the emptiness in her womb. It draws him like gravity toward her. She's there, alone, front row, centre aisle. She smiles, and Hobo looks away.

Take a woman young and bare, he thinks.

"My Lords, my Ladies, my Gentlemen."

The lights dim. Hobo hears the hiss of the dry-ice machines, feels their delicate mist kiss his face. A single bass note rumbles through the top. A lone yellow spotlight stains Whiteface pallid, demonic, otherworldly as he dances out the words.

"For your terrible astonishment, we bring you the ultimate human journey; from life, to death, to life anew. A volunteer, ah yes, you madam, front row centre, please, for one moment only, won't you join the circus?" Whiteface pauses dramatically as the librarian lurches forward. "Though, of course, you should savour it, for it might be your last moment on Earth."

The spotlights widen. There's an altar, now, in the middle of the ring, flanked by a Gothic arch with Neo-Classical stone pillars to the side. There are carvings of ancient Gods, of snakes and ocelots and demons and harpies. There is a curl of smoke, a wisp of intrigue. There's a knife, and a hammer, a goblet for the blood and a golden pail for the organs.

Whiteface leads the librarian to the altar. Her hand shakes as she pulls it to her side and he lays her down. She breathes rapidly.

"Your task, madam, is simplicity itself: to lie still and dream of new life."

Hobo backs away.

36

"The trick, Hobo," whispers Whiteface, as the audience hush and the spotlights close in like hunters. "Now is the time."

Hobo shakes his head. He turns and runs, as fast as his oversized boots will allow. *Hobo!* Whiteface's yell is in his ears, and the bells on his hat tinkle insanely. Hobo runs to his caravan, falling inside and then rising to turn the lock behind him. He leans gasping for breath against the closed door. Tears smear his greasepaint. He rubs his face with his palms. They're red, but not blood red.

She's there, Sunday morning, as the top's flags snap in the breeze and Hobo sits on the canal bank. Hobo hears her librarian shoes upon the gravel behind him. He turns and sees her wince.

"He beat you up?"

Hobo says nothing. One eye is closed, and the other stings in the weak sunlight. His face is puffed and bruised, so much that it hurt even to renew his paint properly this morning. His clown smile sits lopsided on broken lips. His bowtie spins slowly.

The librarian pulls a tissue from her pocket. She leans down to dab at an open wound on Hobo's face. She smells of lavender, fresh and feminine. Her blouse falls forward and Hobo stares. He counts the moles on her breasts, right down to where hidden nipples press against the barest of white lace prisons.

"I would have let you do it," she says. "The trick, I mean, I'd have let you do the trick."

Hobo nods. "Even though it would have killed you?"

She strokes her stomach. "Sometimes, a woman's urges really are that strong."

Hobo knows nothing of women's urges. He knows little of his own urges if he were truthful. He studies the librarian's breasts as they rise and fall, as she continues to dab at his wounds. Hobo's erection unfurls in his baggy clown-pants. He reaches inside her blouse and cups a breast in his palm. The librarian pauses and stiffens, but she doesn't pull away at once.

"I must have a child," she says. She smiles and moves Hobo's hand away. "But not that way. You can't give me a child that way. I've lost too many already, that way."

"Then you want me to do the trick?"

"I do."

"I've seen what it does to a woman."

"You've done the trick before?"

Hobo shivers. "I was born that way. My mother was dead within minutes."

The librarian kisses Hobo gently upon the forehead. She pulls his head into her chest. Hobo nuzzles, her flesh is soft and warm.

"I'm sorry," she says.

Later, in the ring, watched by no one but Whiteface and Mrs Elms, Hobo is tied to a spinning wooden wheel while Ewan the Eyeless throws knives.

Thud... thud... thud...

Hobo flinches; some of those blades land close enough to tinkle the bells on his gowns.

"What to do with him?" says Whiteface.

Mrs Elms looks up from making emus. Her hands are dirty from the earth she moulds. And these crude golems look like no emu Hobo has ever seen, not until Mrs Elms bathes them in a small cauldron of swirling gas and they leap out howling and wailing.

"Drown him," she says. "That's what I do with the emu runts. Drown the damp squibs and the ones that look like they won't go off."

Mrs Elms goes through many emus.

Ewan the Eyeless squints, blindly. "You want I put a knife through his heart, Whiteface?" Ewan throws. The knife thuds against Hobo's chest... handle first. The blow stings last night's bruises awake. "I can do it now, if you want."

Whiteface strokes his chin. "Is this not the dark circus? There are surely more *interesting* ways of ridding ourselves of Dullards and Simpletons."

"I could have him explode," says Mrs Elms. "I could fill him full of fireworks."

Thud! A knife draws a sliver of skin from Hobo's arm. He feels blood pool. "Or I could flail the skin from his body inch by inch."

"Whiteface, please," says Hobo. "I want to do the trick. I wasn't ready, that was all. Let me do the trick tonight. I'm begging you."

"You'll run," says Whiteface. "You'll make the circus look stupid. You'll let me down."

"No, no, I promise."

"Very well," says Whiteface. "There is one last chance. If you fail me tonight there will be no more. Do you understand me, Hobo?"

Hobo nods. "Perfectly, Whiteface."

———

It's dark early. There's a storm on the way from the west. Thunder grumbles in a sullen sky. Hobo waits by the ticket tent, peering out at the gathering crowds. He sniffs the air, smells the tang of rain in the wind, but there's no scent of the librarian.

He picks up one of two books at his feet. *The Fine Art of Pulling Children from Women*. The pages are now dog-eared and worn. They're smeared with Hobo's crude drawings, scribbled pointers and diagrams etched in pencil. Many of the words he's crossed out.

Hobo tosses the book in the bin nearby. He picks up the second book and hides it away in his gowns. Its pages are older, more powerful, and Hobo feels them rustle alive in his pocket.

Whiteface will surely be amazed, he thinks, and turns to enter the top.

It's a subdued performance. It's as if the oncoming storm is a distraction. Mrs Elms' emus won't ignite, try as she might to get them going. They hiss and smoke and whimper and hide. Ewan the Eyeless has taken the ear off a passing bareback rider. Even Whiteface appears edgy and nervous.

Hobo is calm. He sees the librarian front and centre. She sits regally, above all the nonsense of sliced ears and smouldering emus. In Hobo's eyes, she's beautiful.

The trumpets blare. The altar is set. The audience holds its breath.

"My Lords, my Ladies, my Gentlemen," says Whiteface. "Behold the very essence of life itself. For your morbid delectations, and perverted pleasures, tonight our own Hobo will pull a fully formed child from the body of a woman."

Hobo strides out into the ring. He moves with purpose towards the librarian. They both stare. They both nod. She rises and Hobo leads her to the altar. Fires flare to the side as she settles. Thunder rumbles outside. Hobo feels the book's pages bristle in his pocket.

40

"But be warned, Ladies and Gentlemen," Whiteface continues, "that this trick is not for the faint of heart. Be aware, there will be death, tonight. But there will also be life. Such are the two fundamental forces ever entwined."

"You took two books," the librarian whispers to Hobo. He nods and she reaches for his hand. "I checked. I know what other book you took."

"Lie still," says Hobo. "And be quiet."

"But...'

Hobo kneels before the altar. He sees Whiteface watching. His stare is heavy and menacing. There's a tremble of expectation upon Whiteface's lips. Hobo closes his eyes. He prays: to Asmodai, to Lilith, to Beelzebub, to Hubris. In his prayers, Hobo soars through storm-bruised skies. In the curl of distant lightning Hobo sees Beelzebub stir. He watches the Nephilim wake. The dark Gods ride to him on hooves of thunder.

"No, Hobo." Whiteface leaps into Hobo's prayer.

Too late. Hobo grins; there's no going back now. Hobo's serene. He's glad.

"No, Hobo." In the top, Whiteface leaps, but there's fire in the tent, and pterodactyls swoop and cry. Smoke rises against the canvas. Panic fills the crowd, and they shove and push to escape. Whiteface swims against their tide, but the flames are white hot, so even he is pushed back.

"Fool, Hobo," he yells. Whiteface shakes his fist as fire grips the masts and the altar. "Fool, Hobo! You'll kill us all."

As Hobo melts he grins. Greasepaint runs down his face, and skin slips from bone. He stands until muscle and bone becomes dust. When he falls, inward like some surplus tower block, Hobo's ashes plume outward. They sparkle like blue-green stars above the librarian's stomach. And are gone.

"Out! Everyone out!" yells Whiteface.

———————

The books are silent when the librarian throws open the door and steps inside. Her librarian shoes clunk against the stone floor as she strides purposely between the shelves.

She finds *The Fine Art of Pulling Children from Women* lurking back on its shelf. She knows it takes more than fire and magic and dark trysts with devils to destroy such tomes. To its side, set back as if in hiding, the second book Hobo took is there too.

The librarian tugs at the second book's spine. It fights to remain hidden, but no book may defy a librarian for long. She reads the title: *The Dark Wisdom in Returning Oneself to the Womb.*

She rubs her stomach as she reads. She's not *showing* yet, but she feels the baby growing inside her. And she knows this one is holding tight. There'll be no obscene trickle *below* this time. No barest shake of a doctor's head. No fleeting glance of midwife misery.

The baby flutters inside her, and the books gasp.

"Hush," she says, to the books, to the baby, to her own fears. "All will be fine."

In the depths of her womb, Hobo sighs. He's warm, and safe, protected by a loving mother.

And he knows that's all he ever wants.

———————

Steven Pirie

Steven Pirie lives in Liverpool, England with his wife and son. His fiction has appeared in magazines and anthologies around the world. His comic fantasy novel, *Digging up Donald*, published in 2004, has attracted excellent reviews. A second novel, *Burying Brian*, was published in December 2010.

Steve's website is: www.stevenpirie.com

Funeral for King Giggles

Donna J.W. Munro

Giggles died during Toby Jenner's birthday party, twisting balloon three-foot-tall Spidermen for five-year-olds, breathless, his heart stopping as the children cheered.

It's how he wanted to go.

Bobo waited for the coroner to finish up with him and presented proper credentials, collecting his remains, and folding them into a tiny red suitcase while whispering the prayers of clown to settle his ghost into his skin and bones. Without hoop pants and ruffled collar, the white make-up and red mouth Bobo wore shocked the Square Joes working in the gray world morgue, but no clown can bring their dead to the next place without full makeup. How would the spirit tethered there know its kin without the bright colors? The red nose? They'd wander the gray world, lost without the beacons.

Nowadays the beacons are so few, Bobo thought, tucking the red suitcase into the miniature yellow car alongside Jazzy and Jingles, the only others who'd come when he'd gotten the call and spread the news. So few clown faithful packed in.

Funeral for King Giggles

Bobo pushed up his red hair into a point that encircled his head, *a la* the great Bozo, prophet and last king of the clowns.

"Kuma Lisa bless us that Bozo passed before this day," Jazzy said from the backseat beside Giggle's remains. "Bozo's funeral held car after car so full there were broken bones."

"Bless the pain," Bobo intoned. Jingles jingled his agreement, since he was a silent clown.

Perhaps there would be more by the seaside for Giggles' internment that night. But clowns had devolved since the circuses had gone the way of the dodo. Those colorful tents and the life teeming within, the laughs and the thrills had been the greatest beacons for their light, for Kuma Lisa's trickster joy destroyed by Square Joe thinking and the world got grayer without the cheerful tents and clattering, painted trains.

And clown colleges?

Bobo dragged his thoughts back from the humiliation of pitching their ancient craft, their religion for $300 a credit hour and offering a certificate to Square Joes who played at clowning for money. He'd apprenticed to King Bozo back in the days before the TV show. His doomed campaign to create new beacons on the boob tube took off at first, but the black and white television failed to create the magic that a hallowed big-top and a congregation of tumbling clowns circling a ring, pulling rainbow scarves, and silky flower bouquets from their sleeves for the Square Joes to marvel over and laugh their joy out as offerings to sweet Kuma Lisa. And then the corporate Squares bought it out, put in fools in drag rather than honest clowns. Willard Scott, for Kuma Lisa sake! What were they thinking?

Bozo had been a good king; even if he hadn't succeeded he'd tried to preserve them. Light the beacons and open the magic doors. And poor Giggles had to follow in his footsteps, unlucky until the end when even

Ringling Brothers retired to Florida and the Big-Tops were given to the moths leaving him the king of a bunch of trickster refugees. What must the last emperor of the Roman Empire have felt as the world crumbled around him? Poor Giggles.

"What about Smiley? Shouldn't we tell him?" Jazzy asked, his bowing frown paint deepening the teary-eyed gaze that smeared his white make up.

He glanced back and saw Jingles pressed to one side of the car and Jazzy to the other, trying hard not to touch the suitcase holding the king's remains. It wasn't law or even bad luck to take care of the bones of a clown ghost, but neither of them believed they should be the ones protecting them. Superstition or culture? Bobo couldn't tell anymore. He just knew that the boys wanted Giggles' own flesh to carry him to the sea for release to Kuma Lisa.

Bobo nodded that they should go after the boy, but bit back what he'd like to say. Little Smiley didn't go by the name Giggles gave him at birth, his sweet clown name. Since he'd left for a new life, he called himself Kevin and he'd become one hundred percent a Square Joe living in a gray world. Poor Giggles gave him life—a clown born, not made. Kuma Lisa bless him. And he'd given it all up.

"I suppose we should. We owe it to Giggles for his son to see him off," Bobo said.

Jingles shook his bells in ringing approval.

———————

Feet up and leaning back in the cozy leather Lazy-boy, Kevin took a deep, calming breath knowing that he'd be there a while. His fiancée, Judy, took hours to get ready. He smiled as he waited for her to emerge from the bathroom with her makeup perfect and dress just so for a dinner to announce their engagement to friends and family. Well, her friends and family if he was honest, but they'd been so kind and accepting to him. Judy deserved to make a show of it.

She deserved so much.

Kevin waited patiently, enjoying the peace and quiet. The sanity of it all and in that moment, he noticed how sleek his black oxford dress shoes looked, sparking in the light like two glossy panthers. Slim shoes. Easy to walk in. He lay his hand against the tortoiseshell buttons of his suit coat, relishing how small and matched to perfection they were. Ah, the little things.

From the bathroom, Judy's sweet voice muttered about how terrible she looked. How nothing fit right. How he had to be insane to marry such a hideous woman with such a tremendous ass.

Kevin had the sense and training to know a cue when he heard one. He pushed up from his chair and moved into the bathroom behind her, sweeping her into a hug that let him see her in the mirror and cradled the back of her to the front of him where she fit just right.

"Stop talking shit about the woman I love," he growled and bent to nibble her ear.

She giggled, accepting his reassurance, then turned, her gaze sweeping across his face and neck.

"What?"

"You need a touch up," she said, reaching for her foundation.

"What would I do without you?" He asked as stretched his neck to let her work on him.

The yellow mini car pulled up in front of the brownstone on a street that clown work wouldn't have paid for in a million and a half years.

"Wow," Jazzy said from the back of the car.

Jingles rang an appreciative bell, in agreement.

"Yeah," Bobo said, pulling his long legs from around the low steering wheel. "Wow."

He'd seen it before, many times back when Giggles dragged him to watch for Smiley, to see him through the window tightening his Square Joe tie and hugging his gray girlfriend. For the last few years, the two of them had eaten pack lunches sitting in the branches of trees outside of the brownstone's window watching Smiley move within his gray world. How hard it had been for Giggles to see his boy, his gift from Kuma Lisa, cover his colors with gray face paint.

At the top of the brownstone stairs, Bobo's big, flappy shoe hesitated mid-step. Would Giggles even want this? All those times they'd come here, he'd never actually reached out to Smiley after he left the Big-top life and Giggles behind. And Giggles had never done anything to stop him, watching his boy from a distance as he schooled himself in Square Joe ways and got himself a job in finance or some other such invisible-gain, square job. Giggles had been proud enough of him. Told Bobo every time they'd come to watch through the window that he felt glad his boy made his way in the strangeness of the gray world. But how often did Kuma Lisa permanently paint a clown child with her own fox colors? White face, red cheeks, black nose, triangles over and under the eyes. Smiley's colors, no matter how he tried to hide them, went down to the bone.

He knocked once, waited for a few deep breaths to pass, and knocked again. Part of him wanted so badly to run from this "Kevin" thing, but for Giggles, he'd do anything.

Funeral for King Giggles

The door swung open and there he stood, gray as a Joe in the stands stuffing his face with Cracker Jacks.

————————

"Bobo," Kevin said, the word spilling out sideways like it hurt to say. And it did. The old fool stood there in civilian clothes but with his bright red hair peaked out and white paint slathered on his face in his sacred trickster mask. Glancing around him, Kevin saw the tiny clown car, yellow as a daffodil, parked along-side the brownstone's iron gate. Jazzy's sad frown and Jingles' ridiculous red nose pressed against the window its window and he knew something was wrong. Part of him, the part he immediately shoved aside, wanted to slam the door in his old life's face. Why not? He'd done it for the past ten years, metaphorically. Why not literally now? But a little voice inside asked the question that made him speak to Bobo the Clown for the first time in ages. "Where's Giggles?"

————————

Bobo waited next to the car for the boy to tell his fiancée about the funeral, so she could make their excuses while Smiley... Kevin came with them to let Giggles' spirit go on. I took five minutes, but Kevin came out and so did a gal, pretty thing with brown skin and curly hair. A fine gal from a fine family by the way she held her head up high and fixed on her gaze on Bobo and not the folks that came either way on the path between them. She was a gal so used to folks making way that she'd stopped noticing it, but it wasn't a mean thing. Just confidence in her bones that made her no-nonsense. She just needed a red nose and she'd be perfect.

"Mr. Bobo?" She asked, extending her hand for a shake.

"Just Bobo, Miss." He took it and as clowns do and kissed her knuckles, sloppily.

"Stop," Kevin hissed, but she smiled and shook her head at him. He took her hand back, capturing it lightly between his own. "You don't have to go."

"I do. He was your father."

A good gal, Bobo guessed, since she really didn't have to go at all.

In the car, Jazzy and Jingles pressed together into the back of the car with Kevin, who, even after years of square life, was still loose enough to knot himself up small for the clown car bit. Judy sat in front quiet as they made their way to the shore for King Giggles funeral.

———————

At the shore, the sun set in a flare of orange and pink behind them and the gray of dusk crept over the face of the sea, swallowing blue sky and light. Jazzy and Jingles painted a dainty clown doll face on Judy and Bobo handed a make-up remover cloth and some colorful clothes to Kevin, the only child of Giggles, priest of Kuma Lisa and king of the clowns.

Kevin wiped off the flesh color so that the white and red streaks he'd been born with shown in the dark, a beacon. He pulled on a neon green wig, what his hair would look like if he let it go back to natural. He glanced shyly at Judy, wondering what she thought of him like this.

She'd never seen him completely clown. He'd told her early on, just because no make-up ever stayed on forever, but all of this had to be too much for her.

"I look weird," he said to her.

She swooped him up in her thin arms and pressed against him, front to front and they fit so well. "Don't talk shit about the man I love."

Kevin smiled into her naturally wild, curly hair until she pulled away to watch the others set up.

They waited together all night, standing guard for the coming of Kuma Lisa the trickster fox goddess, their maker and keeper who brought dawn and all of the faithful to the next world.

Kevin and Judy ringed around the suitcase with the others, listening to stories of Giggles' goodness. His kindness. His strength.

"Where are all the others?" Kevin asked.

Bobo shook his head, wishing he could tell a lie to the boy so he'd leave with a sweet fiction instead of the truth, but at the edge of the sea, he knew that Giggles' soul waited for the truth to be spoken out loud. That's what funerals were for.

"None of them are here because, King Giggles is more hated than any other clown king."

"What?" Kevin's features crumpled up in confusion and then anger. "He was a good clown."

"It's not his fault that circuses died," Jazzy said. And Jingles shook his head along, bells clapping in protest, since he was a silent clown. "But clowns blamed him. Said that..."

The three clowns glanced at each other, afraid to continue.

"What did they say?" Kevin asked.

Bobo ran his fingers across the underside of his jaw, watching the horizon for the light of Kuma Lisa, the promise that all clowns wait for at the end, but the sky remained pitch black over the sea and he knew he could wait no more or she wouldn't come.

"They say that he's the last king. That he killed the kingdom, letting you go like he did."

Kevin's face stayed blank, but Bobo guessed on the inside he had demons to wrestle with plenty. Judy pipped up in his silence.

"What do you mean, killed? Children go away from their families, sometimes. Most of the time—"

"Maybe in your world, Miss Judy," Bobo said. "The gray world does such things, but in our world, we must have our beacons. Smiley's face... Kevin's... how he was born, was a sign. That's what we all thought. Giggles raised him to be the next king, blessed of Kuma Lisa. But he left us and..."

The sky stayed dark, resisting the sun rise. Paused, Bobo thought, maybe to see what would happen.

Kevin turned to Judy, tears in his eyes. "I didn't mean it. I didn't think it was true."

She nodded and tucked herself into the crook of his arms as he cried.

Freedom isn't ever really a thing we have. We play at it sometimes, but in the end, we are only what we are.

"I'm sorry, papa," Kevin whispered.

And the sky whispered back, *Smiley, my son.*

Judy changed as the sun's first rays fell on her. Poor Smiley held more in his arms than he knew.

Bobo felt his knees fold. He knelt next to Jazzy and Jingles as Kuma Lisa' colors lit the sky, pouring out in waves. Behind them, in the spill of color bursting across the sand, the clowns of New York flowed over the dunes. Hundreds of them. As they came, they fell to their knees before the glory that was the fox goddess, their maker.

She stepped away from Smiley, across the sand, paws never hesitating, head never bobbing as she moved. She knew no one would get in her way because there was confidence in her bones. She padded over to the suitcase that held Giggles, nosing it until it opened and as it did her colors blossomed in the sky.

Behind them, the clowns, kneeling before her, began to chant their words and sing their songs for the passing of Giggles, the king. Their sweet breath warmed the air and stirred the clouds rioting in the sky with festival colors.

"Judy?" Smiley asked.

She trotted back to him, curling up next to him to watch Giggles ascend on the breath of all the New York clowns and wrapped in her colors.

"Kuma Lisa," she said, and turned back into her brown haired, face painted, clown self. "Still love me?"

Bobo watched from where he sat and felt for the boy. So many changes to what he thought he was, but Bobo knew from the second that gal had swished down the stairs and folded up into his clown car that Smiley, Kevin, belonged with her more than anyone belonged anywhere.

"Still love you forever," Kevin nodded and wrapped her in his arms. His triangle eyes crinkled happily. "Call me Smiley."

Donna J.W. Munro has spent the last nineteen years teaching high school social studies. Her students inspire her every day. An alumni of the Seton Hill Writing Popular Fiction program, she has appeared in many magazines and anthologies, including *Syntax and Salt*, *Dark Matter Journal*, *Astounding Outpost*, *Door=Jar*, and *Enter the Apocalypse*. Contact her at www.donnajwmunro.com

Auguste in Spring

Christopher Stanley

There won't be a second curtain call tonight. The moment the red velvet falls, she rushes downstairs towards the darkness. The other actors roll their eyes as she passes. She knows what they say about her—that she's too young and immature. They say she got the part because of her cheek bones and small shoulders. That while they were busy acting, she was busy seducing the audience.

She hurries through the backstage maze, past stagehands and understudies, through the haze of sweat and hairspray, desperate to retreat behind the locked door of her private dressing room. Her shoes bite into her swollen feet. Her corset crushes her ribs. If she doesn't undress soon, she's going to burst out of her costume.

Finally, she arrives at the door with her name on it. She reaches for the handle but another hand closes around hers.

"My darling," he says. "You were fantastic tonight."

She looks up at the director's face, his narrow eyes and the horns of silver hair growing from his ears. She searches his expression for kindness or evidence of a conscience to which she might appeal, and finds neither.

"Another year older," he says, "and more beautiful with every passing day. That was your best performance yet. Eighteen years old and I've already made you a star."

He strokes his fingers over her hip and she recoils without thinking. His eyes narrow further and he moistens his lips with the tip of his tongue.

"I had a bottle of Champagne sent to your room so we might celebrate your success. Together."

He starts to open the door but she stops him, shaking her head.

His expression boils and then cools. "How rude of me," he says. "You mustn't blame me for being impatient. I could never wait for Christmas to … unwrap my presents." He steps away from the door and she wants to cry with relief. "I'll be back shortly. Why don't you slip out of those clothes and make yourself more comfortable."

Inside her dressing room, she leans against the door and listens to his retreating footsteps. The room is little more than a cupboard for clothes racks and boxes of props, but there's a lock on the door she's come to think of as a close friend.

When she's sure he's gone, she steps into the centre of the room. Her clothes are so tight she'll be strangled if she doesn't remove them soon. She kicks at her heels but they won't budge. She leans forward to tug with both hands and it feels like she's tearing the flesh from her bones. Gradually her shoes slip free.

She stands up again and hears a ripping sound as a seam gives on her costume. The clasp behind her back refuses to come undone. She pushes her shoulders back and tries again, but her fingers are slippery with sweat. Another seam rips. Realising it's too late to save the dress; she breathes as much air into her lungs as she can, her ribs rising, her chest expanding. More of the stitching gives and then the clasp pings across the room.

Free at last, she takes a deep, calming breath. She wriggles her toes to get the blood flowing again and notices her feet are five inches longer than the shoes she removed. Her bottom and thighs have swollen too, her tights laddered from thigh to heel on both legs, the elastic of her knickers cutting deep groves in her skin.

She slips into a white towelling robe and goes to the room's only window, which is no bigger than a porthole. Neighbouring buildings block most of the light so she can only see the tiniest sliver of night sky. It's enough. The full moon smiles down at her, its round face reminding her of her father. And his warning.

"After your eighteenth birthday," he'd said. "During a full moon in spring."

At the dressing table, in the light of eighteen naked bulbs, she removes her wig and rests it on the mannequin head. She wipes the blush from her face and the skin beneath is the colour of blood on white cotton. She scrubs harder, scraping until her whole face feels swollen and sore, but the colour remains. Trembling, she strokes the mascara from her eyes and rubs the lipstick from her lips. Without make-up, she's a beefsteak tomato with white-panda eyes and an ivory smile. She peels the wig cap from her head and, where she used to have dark-brown curls, she now has a banana-yellow frizz. Her teeth are different too. Gone are the rows of perfect pearls; her bite has an edge to it that wasn't there before.

Her father worried this would happen. For a few days every month, he was a notorious white-faced clown—the scourge of the theatre district—and he'd hoped she would follow in his oversized footsteps. Red-faced auguste clowns are known to be anarchists or jokers, less sophisticated than their white-faced counterparts. He always thought she was better than that.

She thought he was crazy.

The door handle rattles. "Let me in," whispers the director.

Her skin crawls at the sound of his voice. She looks around the room, wondering where she can hide if he knocks the door down, but there's nowhere big enough. She tries to breathe but her nostrils feel like they've closed up, as though something is trying to force its way out through the front of her face. She panics and the room begins to spin.

"Don't tease me," says the director.

With the heel of her palm she smacks herself on the nose. Hard enough to make her eyes water. A little air gets through.

"I need to see you."

She hits herself again and again, one hand after the other, until her nose splits open like seams of her costume, spilling out the round, yellow pompom underneath. She shakes her head and breathes normally.

"You promised!" says the director, his voice rising in pitch and volume.

She peels her old nose away and drops it in the bin by her feet. The face in the mirror is unrecognisable. Wild, crazy eyes. A nose that would be better suited to a child's bobble hat. A grin so wide it practically kisses her eyebrows, with lips parted to reveal raggedly pointed teeth. Her reflection is a lie. It shows none of what she feels inside: the fear that rattles her stomach, the terror that squeezes her throat.

The director thumps the door with his fist, saying, "Listen, sweetheart, if you value you career you'll treat me with the respect I deserve."

She dreads the director but she needs to know the reflection in the mirror isn't really her. It's a hallucination; a nightmare from which she'll eventually wake up. The director will see the truth. She doesn't want to face him but she can't be alone in her dressing room anymore. Not with that face staring back at her. Not with that smile, which looks like it could kill.

On the other side of the door, she can hear the director pacing; his breath coming in short, impatient gasps. She slides the latch and turns the handle.

"Come in."

The door opens slowly, as though the director expects a fight. She waits in the centre of the room, thinking she would gladly fight him if it meant she wasn't a clown. She could cope with being fired, as long as she could be normal again.

The director sees her and doesn't scream. He doesn't even look shocked, just puzzled. *He's trying to work out why I let him in*, she thinks, *that's all it is*. She steps forwards, relieved, wanting to throw her arms around him, wanting to squeeze her worries away.

As she approaches, the director's hands rise up defensively. Disgust ripples his brow as he retreats into the shadowy corridor.

"No," she says, the word catching in her throat. "Wait! Please!"

The director turns and flees into the maze of backstage passages, bouncing off walls and sliding around corners. She wants to cry but her eyes won't let her. She wants to run in the opposite direction, towards the exit, but her legs won't go. Instead, she follows the director, waiting for him to slip up, knowing it's only a matter of time before she gets her hug.

She has a bone-white smile that says everything will be okay.

Christopher Stanley lives on a hill in England with three sons who share a birthday but aren't triplets. His novelette, *The Forest is Hungry*, was published in April 2019. His short stories have won The Singularity science fiction contest, The Molotov Cocktail's Flash Rage contest and The Arcanist ghost story contest, amongst others. Follow him on Twitter @allthosestrings.

Giggles for Bimbo

N.D. Coley

Why are people so scared of clowns? It isn't the larger than life make-up, the bright red lips or cartoon shoes. It isn't the cartoonish hats or the shiny, baggy pants, or the polyester vests with balls of fabric for buttons, and it certainly isn't because you're all hooked on stories where clowns are demons, space aliens, or serial killers. That stuff is just your way of telling the rest of us that you're scared of us.

And trust us, we know, and we know because we can't hide the fear in our own eyes. Look behind the getups, forget about the gags, ignore all the silly props, and you'll notice one thing in every clown that you meet. We are scared. Terrified. We are prisoners, and every joke that escapes our lips, every pie that hits our faces? These are payments on our existence. We live and die based on the joy we give to others.

Why wouldn't we be afraid, and who wouldn't notice such fear? You're afraid of us because you know how scared we are.

Think about the clowns that you've met. How much do you know about their histories? You might do a background check, but that's only going to weed out the obvious problems: rapists, murderers, pedophiles, and run of the mill sickos. If you could look into the biography of each and every clown you've met, you'd notice a gap, a space where information seems to have gone missing or been erased altogether, and you'd never give it a second thought without another reason to be alarmed. People make mistakes, right? Documents get lost, people forget, and someone who has worked as a salesman and a construction worker and a clown might have a year missing in the mid 90's, but nobody thinks about that. Pad a little more in 1992 and 1994, and the average parent who needs you to settle down a room full of screaming brats won't say a thing about 1993.

Everyone is uncomfortable with clowns. Everyone skips over those little details.

Here's what happens in those gaps, and here's why, whoever you are, I am absolutely scared to death of you and everyone else like you.

———————

My given name was John once, but you can just call me Bimbo. Bimbo the Clown. I was the unwanted child of parents who snorted blow on purpose and had me by accident. When I was seven years old, I went into the living room to tug on my mother's skirt and ask for dinner, but she and pop were face down, on the floor, crisscrossed over each other, blood dripping out of their noses. I remember someone throwing a sheet over them and giving me a cold bacon and egg sandwich to eat, and that's where my childhood memories basically began and ended: a set of dead parents, bacon, and eggs.

Typical right? A boy in and out of foster care, in and out of juvenile halls, in and out of girl's skirts. In and out. In and out. In and out. If I had to piece together memories of my life before I become a clown, I could have squeezed the basics onto an index card. Wake up. Steal something.

Piss someone off. Rinse, rise, and repeat.

Everything changed one year during the annual county fair. I was waiting on some of my friends (if you can call them that) to join me. The night was cool, and all things considered it was a nice evening. I always liked the fair. I enjoyed the oversized light bulbs above the booths, and the games where kids with nice parents (who had them purpose and all) threw balls at wooden monkeys and walked out of the booth with smiles on their faces and giant leopards tucked under their arms. There was something about that place that made me feel like I didn't need a friend, and that the carnival itself was my friend.

I had some time to waste and a few extra amusement tickets in my pocket from the night before, so I took a ride on the Ferris wheel, a rickety old thing with rusted bolts and chipped paint all over. I liked the bucket seats, though, and the way they'd sway when the ride got going up to full speed. Now that I look back I think that sitting in those seats, going round and round, and looking at the carnival from up high? Happiest I have ever been.

I got on by myself and clicked the safety bar shut, and round and round the wheel went. Now, if you like this ride as much as I do, you'll know that the lucky riders get stopped way up at the tip top to allow for other riders to get off. It's a hell of a view. What was strange this time is that nobody was in line, I was the only person on the ride, and the wheel stopped. I sat there for a few minutes. My first thought was relax. No worries. The operator just wants to give you a bit of the view. But I didn't think so. I saw the disinterested look on that kid's face, buried behind a blanket of pimples. He didn't seem the type to look at a punk like me and say yeah. Sure. I think this nice man needs a view.

I shouted hello from above, but the kid just sat there, on a stool, scribbling on a crossword puzzle or something.

And that's when the man in the red suit and bowler hat climbed up the side of the bucket seat and sat next to me. I didn't hear him coming. He just popped up and over the side, swung a lanky set of legs around, and the next thing I knew there he was. His face was round and red. His eyes were narrow and green, almost like tiny bulbs had been screwed in there. He had a thin black mustache that was waxed up and styled into curls. I didn't know what to say. I mean. Would you? As it happened, he spoke first.

Lovely evening, John, yes? May I call you John?

Sure, I croaked. I noticed that my knees were shaking.

All by yourself, I see? No friends to ride this wondrous wheel with?

My pals are late.

Oh late they are. Listen. I don't think you'll be seeing them again. Something a little birdie just told me. A robbery at the bank in town. The one next to the hardware store. Things went terribly wrong. Two injured tellers. An injured cop, and three suspects, all with fatal gunshot wounds. You really should pick friends who are more careful.

What the. Who. Who are you?

Oh that's not important right now.

Get out. I've tossed people bigger than you from higher places.

Hmmmm, maybe so, but I wouldn't in this case.

Why not?

The man reached into his coat pocket and pulled out a Manila envelope. He fumbled at the opening with his bony fingers and slipped out a series of Polaroid photographs. They were all different angles of the same shot. They pictured a red tricycle, mangled in the middle of the street. There was a smear of blood next to the tricycle, the smear crossed by a set of skid marks. Off to the side, a cracked wrist watch lay face down in a glob of blood.

I looked at the man stupidly.

Well what? I asked.

You don't remember? I seem to think you know something about a little joyride that you took in a stolen Plymouth some months ago. It was great fun, though there was the matter of the child in your path. Somehow, you lost your watch in the incident. Good thing I recovered it first! My, oh my. Do you remember setting fire to the car later, behind the city dump? What a mess!

I looked at the man and searched for the memory. I knew that he was telling the truth. Bits of the incident came back to me in tatters and vanished again, down the alcohol soaked caverns of my mind.

Was the boy ok? Did he survive?

The man pulled out a pocket watch, flipped it open, nodded, and closed it.

Now that, John, I don't know. I only go as far as I need to know. What I do know is that the authorities would probably love a tip off to the incident, regardless of what happened.

I opened my mouth to ask if he knew the boy's name, and then thought better of it. I knew he had decided that right now, I wouldn't know.

So what's next? I asked.

Well, that's entirely up to you. Here's what's going to happen. In just a few moments, I'm going to see to it that this ride you're on goes round and round again. When you reach the bottom and get out, there will be a blue box, about the size of a sheet of paper, in the bin where people store their personal items before getting on the ride. Take that blue box, open it, and do what it says? Nothing. These pictures stay with me.

And what if you have an accident before then?

You're going to go there again, eh? You see, the pictures I have aren't the only copies. Your actual watch, the finest in rip-off timepieces, finger prints and all, is in a safety deposit box, and I did this thing this morning. I said to my lawyer: If I should happen to fall to my death from the top of an amusement ride, the items in question are to be sent to such and such, along with the following letter.

I looked at him blankly. I look into those green eyes. The colors in them swirled, and his gaze cut into me. I swear to God if I had the choice between burning in hell and having that stare locked on me, stripping me down, cutting me in half? I'd take hell. I had no choice in this. None. I nodded.

Bravo! He said, Bravo!

The ride jerked into action again. I looked down to see that yes, there was indeed a box deposited in the bin near the gate, and when I brought my eyes back up to ask the man in the red suit and bowler hat a question, he was gone.

Late that evening, I marched as fast as I could, underneath a dark sky and a heavy rain, under the bridge where my crew and I would sit and get stupid. They weren't there, and I suspected that a glance at the local news would tell me that the man was right—they were dead. Gunned down in a stupid attempt to take down people smarter, faster, and stronger than them. Come to think of it, I don't even think I learned their names. Not something you need to know to get high.

I dried off the box with a nearby rag. It was sturdy and hand carved, painted in a powder blue with black streaks. The strange thing is that there wasn't a seam, or a hinge, so it didn't seem like a box at all, but a hunk of wood. I looked it over and discovered, on the bottom of it, two slots that look like thumb prints. I placed my thumbs in and pressed, and the top of the box began to crumble, like fine grains of sand. Hell. I know this sounds nuts, but it's the truth. I'd swear on my mother's grave if she meant something to me.

What was left in my hands was a rolled up piece of paper, held together by a red ribbon. I slid the ribbon off and unrolled the paper. In it was a black and white drawing of a clown. He stood over a crowd of screaming, impatient children. He held a pie in his right hand, and with his left hand he seemed to point to. Well. Me. His face was intent. Maybe borderline sinister. His red lips, large and protruding, were forced into a deep frown.

Underneath the clown was a handwritten note: Big Top Pizza. Tomorrow. 4:00 PM.

And that was it. But Big Top Pizza? This was the local version of Chuck E. Cheese. Only think smaller and more disgusting. It really was a shit hole. The pizza was always cold, the soft drinks were always flat. Half the arcade machines were turned off, and the one's that actually powered up usually had a button missing. Big Top Pizza was where your parents would have a birthday party for their rotten children.

Big Top Pizza had also been closed down for years. Some poor sap got food poisoning form their pizza and, while vomiting at home, fell down his stairs and broke his own neck. Swear to God. There were 8 other cases of food poisoning the same night, with no fatalities. Big Top got sued, the owner closed up and headed for anywhere but here, and that was that. Now it's only used by teenagers looking to have awkward sex and drink malt liquor.

I looked at the paper again. Big Top Pizza, I said. Why not.

I spent the next morning wandering the fair grounds. I thought that I might, if I looked around enough, see the man in the red suit and bowler hat, but there was hardly anyone around. A few security guards sat on a stoop and smoked cigarettes while playing Gameboy. Gusts of wind blew empty bags of popcorn and soda cups about. I walked past the booths that would later be filled with games and stuffed animals and annoyingly happy attendants. I approached the Ferris wheel and gazed into the empty cars. The structure creaked a little in the wind, and the way that it swayed made it seem unsafe, like a death trap fitted with bucket seats.

The ride operator was in for his shift. He had a spray bottle in one hand and a dirty rag crammed into his back pocket. He approached one of the cars, scrunched his nose, and recoiled. Vomit. I could smell it too. That was the way of things for him. People would ride something that made you wobble and go up and down and backwards, get off, board the giant wheel, and puke. The operator sighed.

Excuse me, I said. He turned.

You're early. The ride's not open yet. Come ba—

No, no. I just had a question.

Alright.

Did you notice anyone yesterday dressed. All weird and shit?

You don't get around this fair much, do you? That's half the people who come in.

No no. You would have noticed. Trust me. Bright red suit. Bowler hat. Creepy ass mustache. He was on the ride with me yester— Never mind. Does this dude sound familiar?

Nope.

I thanked the kid and strolled out of the fairgrounds. Was I nuts? I'd read shit about how too much booze and the wrong kinds of drugs will shrink your brain, drill holes in it, cause hallucinations. I figured what was left of my own mind would be good for science or whatever.

God, I whispered to myself. This is stupid. Stupid, stupid.

I took out the flyer for Big Top Pizza, crumpled it, and tossed it into the open mouth of a porcelain clown mounted over a garbage can.

I walked on, tired, slightly dragging my feet. I was hungry and even the smell of stale popcorn and old grease awakened eagerness and pain in my stomach. I stopped and rested my elbows on a corn dog stand; the booth was empty, all lights were off. My eyes fixed on the menu and I licked my lips—there were pictures of perfectly browned French fries smothered in curls of ketchup, burgers topped with bacon and lettuce and melted cheese, frothy chocolate milkshakes and fried clumps of dough and powdered sugar. My stomach growled, and I groaned. I pressed my hands to my temples and shut my eyes. I hadn't eat'n in days. Time to grab an empty cup, a cardboard sign, and hit the interstate. Do my thing.

I opened my eyes, and there was a man, maybe 50 or so, bald and broad shouldered. He was dressed in a fairgrounds uniform. He grinned a crooked smile and shouted over his shoulder.

Hey! Order for John ready! Order for John!

He spun around and returned with a tray with a silver platter on it.

I looked at him blankly.

Here ya go, kid. Special order. Just for you!

I placed three fingers on the platter's lid. I did so slowly. I think I half expected the damned thing to bite. Underneath the platter, in the middle of the plate, was just about the most gorgeous hamburger I had ever seen. The patty was thick and topped with melted cheddar and onion straws. The bun was a perfect golden dome. BBQ sauce dripped down the sides and onto the plate. And I know what you're thinking here! Doesn't this seem a bit strange to you, being served outside of business for something that you didn't order, and by a man who shouldn't be there?

Let me tell you this: You get hungry enough and everything makes all the perfect fucking sense in the world.

I picked up the burger with two hands. I jammed that sucker into my mouth and, for a moment, my mind was wrapped around the idea of my teeth, tearing into the meat, releasing those juices onto my tongue, sloshing around a mix of onion and sauce and cheese. Bits of buttery brioche broke off and went sliding down my throat, and with each bite my mouth became greedier and greedier.

And that's when I noticed that the taste in my mouth was more like used wads of chewing tobacco, discarded banana peels, stale bread and old popcorn, all coated with a coating of garbage juice. My teeth kept mashing, but it wasn't through bread or meat. It was paper. I gagged, reach grabbed a curled up leaf of paper and pulled it out of my mouth. It seemed to resist a little and stick to my tongue and gums on the way out.

I unrolled the paper, and there was the picture of the clown again, and the handwritten note. Only this time there was some added text at the bottom:

We don't want to miss you!

I folded the paper this time, carefully, and tucked it away in my front pocket, and when my eyes returned to the booth it was empty and quiet and the bad man in the uniform was gone.

Big Top Pizza looked especially shitty, and which was an impressive feat, even for a place that had been closed for years. The windows had long since been busted and boarded over with plywood, though most of the window coverings dangled by a single nail, having long been pried open by bums like me in search of shelter. Outside the doors, flanking the entrance on both sides, were statutes of Pippin the Clown, the official mascot, and his sidekick, Milo the Mouse. They were oversized figures. The paint on them was chipped, and patches of rust covered the surface in the likeness of a skin disease. I passed between the two, afraid to look into their eyes, and especially afraid to let my shoulders touch them. I sped up quickly and snuck into the wide-open doorway.

The inside was dark and smelled musty. I took a few steps forward, and not being able to see at all, yelled into the blackness.

Hello? Hello anyone there? I'm here. It's me. You. Uh. You didn't miss me!

Three stage lights burst onto an animatronic stage in front of me, where life-sized models of Pippin and Milo, decked out in fur and costume, awaited their animatronic orders. Both of them were covered in cobwebs, and Milo was missing an eye. I stepped forward, slowly, until I was at the stage, and at arm's length I reached out and put a hand on Pippin. As my fingers touched his arm, Pippin and Milo jolted awake and started waving their arms from side to side. Their bodies shook and creaked. Their chins rose, and their eye's blinked. A slow, out of tune calliope song erupted from a speaker behind them. Milo cocked his head in my direction and spoke, his jaw chomping out of rhythm with his words. His words were high pitched and distorted, almost like he was being played from an old record.

Well wheeee P-P-P-PPin! What-oly-doo! What do you think we have here?

Milo my Milo! This is our good pal!

OOOOO yes. Yes. He's our special friend who shoots powder up his nose!

Yes!

He's our best bud who guzzles deeee-licious drinks from a big brown bag!

Yes, Milo my boy, yes!

And he's our newesttttt

Yeesssss?

Giggles for Bimbo

Our brand spanking nee-awwwwww

Well?

Clown!

A horn sounded and a burst of confetti descended from the ceiling—thin, square bits of red and white paper. The rain of confetti came down thicker and faster until it was a blizzard and I could only a see a red and white. The distorted voices of Milo and Pippin whispered to each other and the whispers turned into growls and the growls turned to snarls. Then the snarls were whispers again, followed by a faint chuckle, and the whispers ceased.

The shower of confetti lightened, and the animatronics were gone, covered by two leather covers. Between the puppets and covers stood the man in the red suit. His hat was in his hand, revealing a head bald except for the center. In the center, his hair was styled into a spiral, like the horn of unicorn. It was a twisted pattern of green and blue. The man fiddled with his mustache and smiled.

I knew you'd see this my way! John, no, no. We can't call you John anymore. That simply wouldn't do. You need your clown name! Your *real* name.

I exhaled and thought about whether my eyes showed how afraid I really was.

Look, Buddy. I. I've done some shit to my mind over the years, so if its ok with you I'm just gonna click my heels three times and go—

Shush, shush! What I need is a name. A silly name. A stupid name. You do know that clowns must be called something funny and playful and ridiculous.

Ok. I'll play along. Call uh. Boz—no. Uh. Bimbo. Yeah. Call me Bimbo.

Bimmmbo! Bimbo! I like it! He yelled slapping his knee. Now, just have a seat at the table over there. Don't mind the rats. Shoo them away with your feet if you need to.

Sit why?

While we wait for your clothes to arrive... You certainly aren't dressed like Bimbo the Clown now, are you?

I rolled my eyes.

No, I said. I guess not. But time out. You mind explaining why I'm apparently a clown all of a sudden? I some asshole to you?

My, my, Bimbo.

Explain this shit or I walk.

Now, now. You know I have the power to share some fun facts about you!

Talk or I walk. Prison would be an upgrade.

Of course! Of course Bimbo. Do you know any clowns?

Depends on what you mean by clown.

Nobody wakes up and decides to be a Clown, Bimbo. They are, shall we say, brought into service. Tsk. Tsk. I'm very sorry to say that there's really no other way. Too many children aren't given laughter, so I step in and fill the need. Clowns are my stock and trade, though we do have other ways.

So you're like a draft. For clowns.

That's right. You would be shocked, well maybe not you. But most people would be shocked at how few grownups would go out of their way to make children smile. I've kept records!

A picture of the bodies of my parents flashed in my mind.

Doesn't surprise me, I said.

Of course not, Bimbo! Part of the reason why you were chosen.

So now what? Time to send me to a birthday party? Honk my nose? Smash a pie my face?

Precisely, but there's a little more to this.

He reached into his coat pocket and produced charm, a ruby about the

73

size of a quarter, cast in silver and fastened to a chain. The ruby glowed and pulsed at its center.

When you are out an assignment, he continued, you will keep this snug against your breast. Don't forget it. Don't harm it. Don't lose it. Think of it as a trap of sorts—a way of catching energy and emotion—if you bring it back and it has turned the color of an emerald green, we know that you have done your job. If it is still red? No good. No good at all.

What happens then?

He twirled one of the curls in his mustache and snapped his fingers.

Leon! Bring him out! Quick, quick now!

A spotlight came on with a loud click, illuminating a stage on the side of the room. Two men emerged from the darkness, one dragging the other's cuffed hands by a rope. The man in front was tall and burly. He wore all black, and his muscles broke the seams of his clothes. His head was covered in a black cloth with two eye slits.

The man he pulled behind him was whimpering. He was short and chubby, and was an awkward fit for the red and green stripped clown suit that struggled to fit over his gut. His mouth was gagged with a rainbow colored handkerchief. He whimpered and jerked his head, which looked awkward and egg shaped. He wore a tiny top hat with a tiny flower. The man bit his lips and sobbed and howled through the gag. I could still make out his words.

Hey hey! I'm sorry God I'm sorry dear Jesus I'm sorry give me another chance just once more chance.

The spotlight flicked off. I heard more rustling and wailing. The light clicked on again.

The man in black stood over the clown, who was now looking out, face forward, from the gallows. At first I was confused because I didn't see a noose, but some glimmers of light above the head of the clown told me what I needed to know. There was a noose, after all, and it was made out of something thin—maybe piano wire.

The spotlight went dark, followed by more grunting and the sound of shuffling.

The stage lit up again, and the clown was scrambling to keep his feet on a narrow, wobbly stool. His eyes bulged as he reached for the wire noose against his neck. I thought that his eyes would burst and tumble out of their sockets. I imagined a string of slime and nerves and blood resting against his cheek, but his eyes just bulged and bulged and did not pop out.

The stage went dark, and I heard something that sounded like leather stretching mixed with spitting mixed with groans and gurgling noises.

The light came on, one last time. The executioner stood, his arms crossed and head up straight. The man in the red suit snapped his hands, and the man in black departed the stage and went into the darkness to his right. The clown's body hung limply from the razor thin noose. It had cut through his neck and windpipe, peeling back layers of deep red and white pitches. His throat, dripping with blood, curled up into a flap of skin. The clown's eyes did not bulge any more, but were wide and motionless. He still looked afraid.

The man in red put a hand on my shoulder. His face was solemn.

I hate to have to show you that, but I have been at this game for a long time, and this is the only way to get the very best of out of my troops. I trust you will understand.

I wondered whether I was dreaming, but I didn't think so. Whenever I see crazy shit like that in my dreams, I scream in the dream, and then I wake up and scream some more. Sometimes things are so horrible that the safest thing to do is stay quiet and look normal. I nodded at the man in red.

Giggles for Bimbo

Off you go, Bimbo. On your way out of the building there will be a burgundy suitcase with your clown name, your real name, engraved on it. In it, you will find everything you need, including your schedule for your probationary period. You'll find a clown car in the parking lot, too. It may look absurdly tiny, even too small for a child, but get in. You will fit. I promise. And remember, keep the pendant around your neck, nice and secure against the breast. We will know if you did your job well. We always know.

The next afternoon, I found myself dressed from top to bottom in a baggy suit with large purple and yellow polka dots. I had clown shoes on my feet, and thick white gloves that made my fingers look like heavy links of sausage. My reflection in the mirror looked back at me with disgust. I did, to be fair to my reflection, look like shit. My makeup settled into the bags under my eyes and only made them look deeper. My hair was greasy and starting to knot in places. My teeth were the color of pale yellow, like bits of wallpaper that had taken in decades of cigarette smoke. I took a deep breath, pressed my hand against my chest to make sure that the charm was there, and stepped out of the bathroom.

A circle of children sat on the floor, arms crossed, and quiet. In the center of the circle, a little girl with blonde hair sported a paper cone hat. The room was full of 6 year olds, and not one of them made a sound. Every last one of them picked me apart with their eyes. They yawned. They learned forward. They ran single fingers through the carpet and drew shapes, but nobody peeped.

I honked my nose.

Hidey-Ho! K-K-Kidos! I'm Bimbo! Bimbo the silly clown! Hello!

The children groaned hello in a long, monotone drawl.

Goodness golly, I chirped, squeezing a faint honk from my nose. Goodness me it seems that we have a birthday girl! What's your name little one?

The little girl stood up, removed her cone hat, and crinkled it. Her arm shot out to the side in accusation to her parents, who hid in the corner, slumped over and defeated.

Mom! Dad! I told you I don't like clowns! I wanted a princess! That is not a princess.

I removed my hat and blew up a pink balloon. I tied it off in the shape of a circle and placed it on my head.

S-S-S-See! I am a princess, I yelled, spitting with each syllable.

The children groaned in unison. One boy, a fat little shit who was bursting out of a stripped polo, his gut swaying side to side, stood up, turned his back to me, and pulled his pants down, reveling two flabby cheeks that looked like dinner rolls. In a moment the children were all on their feet, slinging insults, jeering, pointing, and tossing junk toys and pieces of hard candy from their gift bags.

I grabbed my suitcase and went through the front door. It shut behind me with a bang, followed by clicks and clacks of multiple locks sliding shut.

It went like this, house after house, for the entire afternoon and into the next day. One kid kicked my feet out from behind and stole my shoes. Another kicked me directly in the knees, and then the groin, while all of the other children smashed cupcakes into my collar and sleeves. I wiped chunks of icing out of my eyes and ears and pulled bits of devils food out of my nostrils. Each door slammed behind me, almost in rhythm. Nobody laughed. Nobody apologized. Nobody said goodbye.

And the pendant on my neck did not show a trace of green.

The next time I stepped in the clown car, the man in red was sitting the passenger seat. He did not sound pleased.

Bimbo I know you're new around here, but you're certainly not showing me that you learn quickly.

I closed my eyes and nodded.

Sorry, boss. I'm not funny. I can't make them laugh.

He howled and slapped his knee. Who, he said, fighting down giggles, said that you had to be funny in order to make someone laugh? Improvise. Adapt. I can't wait forever for you to get it right. Lotsa bums like you are in talent pool for this. You're as replaceable as the next sap.

————————

My next stop was a perfect little rich home, in the perfect part of town, with perfect little rich kids dressed in perfect little outfits from Eddie Bauer and Nordstrom's. The children sat on their living room floor, their bored eyes set on me, waiting to see how I would begin. Behind them, rows of distracted parents got lost in their cell phones. One woman in a blazer whispered insults into a wireless headset and paced back and forth.

Hi-ya kiddos! I said, you know what's not funny?

The children looked at me in silence.

This pie that I was gonna put in my face. That's not funny! Or this flower that shoots water. Funny? Yeah right! Not funny at all! Hoodely hoo! Not funny. Not funny! I'll tell you what's funny, though, look here!

I reached into a canvas satchel and produced two 12 inch action figures— one in the likeness of a cowboy, a rugged man in denim overalls, a red shirt,

78

and a brown hat. The other one, a classic damsel in distress model, wore a pink dress that poofed out at the bottom. I held the dolls up and gave them voices, a nice, deep gruff one for the cowboy, and something high pitched and soft for the damsel. I made them talk, laugh, and argue with each other. I shook the doll cowboy violently and laughed, and in an instant, I opened up my mouth and bit off its head . My teeth tore into the plastic. I spit it out and stomped on it, and with the damsel in my other hand, I cried out in my best damsel voice.

Ohhhh no! Oh no what has happened to you my brave—

And then I bit off the head of the damsel. I made a loud gnawing sound and chewed the dolls head. I spit it out, and I stomped on it and I stomped on the head of the cowboy.

And the children all laughed. They became a roaring sea of giggles. They doubled over and flung out their arms. They wiggled and arched their backs and put their hands over their mouths. One boy took up the corpse of the damsel and starting ripping off the arms and legs. He tossed the torso into the air, which was attached by several sets of tiny hands. It bounced among the crowd of clawing, howling children and disappeared. The cowboy followed.

The parents, for their part, took little notice. The severed arm of the cowboy hit one father in the head. He scratched his nose and continued texting. One mom stood, a glass of red wine in hand, and whispered mischievous things to another mom. They giggled and sipped their drinks and patted each other on the shoulders. Meanwhile, I marched through the crowd of children, like a general in the days where generals were out in the middle of battle, barking orders to the children. Yes! Kill him. Get her. Get her good. Stop it. Twist it. Snap it! That's a good boy! That's a good girl. I yelled, and the children laughed. They destroyed, and they laughed, and when I thought they might be out of energy, I reached into my satchel and pulled out 4 more dolls and flung them into the crowd. The dolls vanished almost immediately, like a hunk of bloody meat into the mouth of shark, and for several more minutes it was a room filled with joy and laughter. Plastic arms and tiny hats and shoes flew about.

The children were soon spent of energy, and all of them seemed to have enjoyed themselves. But I noticed that there was this boy, off in the corner, huddled up and crying. I was bowling a near perfect game, save for him. I approached and put a hand on his shoulder.

You ok, little boy? What's the matter. Uncle Bimbo can help.

He sniffled. No, no you can't. I don't like your game. I'd rather have pies and silly noises. I want knock knock jokes. I want doggies to be made into balloons. This isn't nice.

It's ok, I said, putting my hand on his shoulder. They are just toys. Just piece of plastic.

The boy let his hand drop to his right calf, where he knocked on it. It made a hollow sound.

Like the plastic on me? Is this what's going to happen to me? I have a plastic leg. Just like that cowboy and his friend. He sniffled.

No, no, it's ok. Your friends know that the toys are toys and that you are you.

No they don't! I got knocked over when I was trying to get away. I did. And then a big fat boy stepped on it, and a mean girl did too, and now there's a crack in it and I can't stand up and my parents are going to kill me.

I rose and tapped one of the wine guzzling moms on the shoulder. She jumped a bit, perhaps as if she had just seen me for the first time that day. I pointed at the boy and started to talk, but she stopped.

Oh don't worry about Timothy there, she said with a hiccup. He'll be ok. Poor thing. Hasn't been the same since his accident earlier last year. Someone. Some drunk just clobbered the poor thing when he was on his tricycle. The poor child was lucky to be alive, I'll tell ya. Lost his leg, though, and the doctors had to give him a fake one. And his parents, bless them, won't spend the money on the best ones, the metal ones, so they make him hobble around on that thing. It really is a tragedy. Parents these days.

The boy sobbed and the parents carried on, talking and texting and slurping their booze, and the rest of the children returned to gentle play with each other until the birthday boy signaled that it was time for cake, prompting a single file march up and out of the war zone. Timothy stayed in the corner and wept.

I didn't say anything, and I couldn't be sure, but somehow I knew. I wrapped my arms around that child and picked him up, and a held up close to me, making his shoulder wet with my tears. I rocked him gently, smearing my makeup onto his jacket, until he was asleep, and carried him into the dining room.

There children were seated, some on their asses and some on their knees, smashing cake down with their palms. They smeared it through their heads and cackled. They flung gobs of it at each other, at their parents. They pressed it into the rug and the furniture, and the way they laughed and laughed made my stomach turn in circles. I fixed my eyes on one child, who I decided might as well have been the child who stepped on poor Timothy's leg, and yelled.

Shut up. All of you. Shut. Up!

The boy on the other end of my gaze burst into tears. The girl next to him started crying, and the domino effect took over until every last child seemed scared and distressed. They picked up their forks and slowly made attempts to put cake into their mouths like good little kids should do.

The pendant against my chest burned. I lifted the chain up with my finger, just in time to see the charm, which had turned fully green, just as the man in red had said, turn back into a glowing, red ruby. The more the children cried, the more the charm changed and the more it burned.

I set Timothy down and left the house. Moments later, the door behind me slammed, followed by the clicks and clacks of locks. Nobody thanked me. Nobody said goodbye.

There was a note on the seat of the clown car. It had a picture of gallows and a thin noose, and a caption that read:

So close! So Close! Now do that again at the next house, but get out before you screw it up!

And here I am, off to the next house. When I was inside the last one, holding little Timothy and telling him it was going to be ok, someone made it their job to leave some stock in my backseats: new sets of action figures and dolls, little toy weapons and tiny toy torture devices, and sealed packets of red liquid that I took to be fake blood. I was all ready to go

I do not need to be funny to make someone laugh. I don't need to tell a joke to amuse.

Why are people so afraid of clowns? Because clowns, like so many out there who jest and entertain and tell stories, know the things that entertain, and it terrifies the clowns. People are afraid of clowns because clowns are afraid of them.

I am ready for my next stop, which I know will need to be my first stop among many, at least if I want to live long enough to tell you about them. If I, or any other clown, comes knocking at your door to make your children smile, or say things that are corny or silly, or even a bit horrifying, all I beg is that you laugh. There are, after all, a shortage of grownups who truly wish to make children happy.

N.D. Coley (MA, English, University of Pittsburgh) is currently an English composition instructor for The University of Pittsburgh at Greensburg and the University of Phoenix. His work has recently appeared in *Shotgun Honey*, *Close 2 the Bone*, *Indiana Voice Journal*, *Corner Bar Magazine*, *Grotesque Quarterly*, *Jakob's Horror Box*, *Massacre Magazine*, *Crack the Spine*, and *Funny In Five-Hundred*. In his spare time, he laments the human condition, reads depressing literature, plays with his son and daughter, and irritates his wife. You can irritate him at ndcoley1983@gmail.com

Being Funny Is a Serious Business

Roger Jackson

Being funny is a serious business.

You'll never find a clown—at least, not one worth his or her greasepaint—who'll tell you otherwise. I'm not talking about the weekenders, the ones who bring their balloon animals and card tricks to enliven a children's party then go back to the rat race for the rest of the week, or the ones who culturally appropriate our craft for the fancy dress shindig or the Halloween festivity. No, I'm talking about the ones that, every time they look in the mirror, even after the last of the greasepaint has been swept away, can still see the crimson at their lips or the ghost of an inky tear, or the mask of pale powder somehow always lurking beneath the façade of their face. The ones born with slapstick in their veins, a nervous system woven from cotton candy and a squirting flower where their heart should be.

It's not a life you leave behind. Like a priest or a hitman, you live your life with secrets and you're chained forever to your history, even when you try to consign the days of collapsing cars and custard pies to the rearview mirror. You are born to entertain, until the last of your breaths. Every true clown knows that, and there are very clear consequences

85

for those who decide to pack away their oversized shoes and their crimson nose and move on.

Have you ever been to a fairground? I bet you have. Try to remember. Imagine yourself standing on the pale, dry dirt, feeling the heat bleed through your shoes. Imagine the stalls full of trinkets and stuffed animals that you *have* to have. There's bunting between the stall's sloping canvas roofs, fluttering in the breeze between the gentle dance of helium-bloated balloons, and there's sunlight on the chipped and cheery paintjob of the big wheel, the faded velvet of the curtains that lead into the fortune-tellers tent, and the grinning neon skulls of the Ghost Train, all of it ingrained with the dust of the thousand towns the fairground has visited before yours.

Remember the lure of the hotdog stall, the mouth-watering smell of crisping onions, the sweet kiss of candy apples in the air, and imagine that you can hear the distant roar of the rollercoaster, the shrieks of terrified joy, and the music that follows you everywhere, a patchwork of jolly organ tunes and the rock songs of your youth booming from the rides, a strange harmony that shouldn't work, but does. Laughter slaloms between the tents, chased by running children, and somewhere there's the thud of a mallet against rubber, and the cheers and jeers when someone manages to ring the bell on the high striker.

So many sounds, but sooner or later you'll find your way to the only one that matters, the one I want to whisper into your ear about.

Stand ten feet away and you can hear the clown's laughter, crackling through the speakers implanted into his glass-fronted booth. You recall an urban myth that the peals of mirth for such things are ancient recordings from Victorian asylums, and watching the mechanical clown rock back and forth on his golden throne, his eyes wild, his mouth locking and unlocking, you could well believe the tale.

Stand five feet away and you can see that the clown is old, maybe the oldest thing in the fairground, peeling greasepaint and threadbare silk, blood-coloured rust at the corners of his clockwork lips. His laughter shrieks through the speakers. His mighty clown shoes tap with glee, and you notice the carpet of dead flies at his feet. At six inches away, you're close enough to touch the scratched, fingerprint stamped glass of the booth now but no, you don't want to do that.

If you were six inches inside the glass, you'd realise that it was soundproof, and that you could hear screams. You'd smell the coppery, stale air within the booth, feel it moving in cold currents across your skin as the clown hurls himself to and fro on his throne. You'd find the clasp at his neck that secures his fraying collar and unlock it, peeling back the silk to expose a skeleton of corroded artificial limbs and oil-choked cogs and metal rods, like some strange funhouse autopsy.

Look closer, and you'd see the pale skin peeking out between the metal, realise the thin arms and legs that have been slipped into the hollow prosthetic limbs. The clown would thrash in protest at your intrusion, the red smear of his smile snapping open and closed, the screams from the mouth within trapping itself inside the booth, inside your head, inside your heart.

You'd fumble with the clips that hold his face to his skull, white paint unrolling beneath your fingernails, and are his metal features twisting towards you now, that mouth trying to bite at your clawing fingertips? Maybe.

At last, that mask would fall, clattering to the blanket of flies, and you'd see my face, the clown who could never leave, even when the laughter stopped. You'd see the eyes that had begged for mercy, that had wept when the request to forsake the life was denied, and the sentence passed. You'd see that my mouth was screaming between loose, haphazard stitches of brightly-coloured twine, my lips frayed and torn by the sharp edges of a clockwork smile.

That's what you'd see if you were inside the booth, or even what you might somehow sense if you thought to approach it, but all around you the fairground sings with light and speed and delighted screams, and the air is magical with the scent of cotton candy and hotdogs. There's a hand in yours, squeezing gently, and your heart races with the promised thrill of a stolen kiss, and so you walk away from the booth and its undying mechanical gaoler, the screams of its latest captive forever unheard.

Being funny is a serious business, and once you're in it, you're in it for life.

Roger Jackson's stories have appeared in several magazines and anthologies, including *Equilibrium Overturned*, *The Flashes of Darkness*, and *Manifest Reality*, as well as being broadcast on UK radio.

His novella *Cradle of the Dead* is available from Bloodbound Books.

A Mime Is a Terrible Thing to Waste

Christopher Degni

First day of mime class was always a strange and wonderful experience. Massimo sized up the set of strangers warming up in the retrofitted space. Most of the participants didn't know what they were getting themselves into. Some were straight off the street, people who found Massimo's ad in the back of the townie weekly. Others came as referrals from the circus arts school where Massimo used to teach. It was always clear which set of people was which.

"While we're stretching, let's go around the room and say a bit about why we're interested in mime."

The students each said a few words, nothing Massimo hadn't heard before. Looked like fun, rounding out the circus arts, strengthening their core. Didn't really know. Massimo subtly skipped over his own story, but there was a fifty-fifty chance someone would call him on it, if previous classes were any experience.

"What about you?"

Massimo hated this part.

"The artistry—" he began.

A Mime Is a Terrible Thing to Waste

The air conditioner roared and sputtered, and at the same time, a young woman burst through the door. She wore leggings and a loose shirt, like she was ready for an exercise class, but they already had everyone Massimo was expecting. At least she spared him having to tell his story.

"Are you lost?" asked Massimo. The class continued their stretches. He would have asked her why she signed up for the class, but then the lens would turn back onto him after she gave her answer, so he was willing to leave it a mystery.

She stood just inside the door, staring at Massimo, the rest of the class brought to a halt. Was the AC getting even louder, or did it only appear that way, with nothing else for Massimo to put his attention on? The woman's eyes narrowed and glinted, a momentary look of anger before tears welled at their corners. Last thing Massimo needed was a crying student.

"Come in," he said.

She joined the others on the mats. As she walked across the room, the skin on the back of Massimo's neck prickled. She moved in an alien way, at slant angles that Massimo felt in his stomach, like her body was put together differently from the standard-order human being. Watching her physically hurt Massimo, so he avoided it as best he could. She likely wouldn't be back next time anyway.

Every time he did glance at her, though, she was observing the other students, like a baby watching adults, absorbing their every movement.

Massimo shook out a shiver.

She chose a mat next to Emily. The new woman watched her intently, but Emily in her boat pose seemed unaware she was being examined. The other students returned to their own warm-ups, the novelty of this new presence having worn off, but Massimo surreptitiously monitored the situation between the unnamed woman and Emily.

Emily's eyes remained closed, at first, but the unnamed woman stared at her intently, and the muscles in Emily's face began to twitch, her eyes moving furiously behind their lids, almost like she was trying to open them but unable. Her breathing picked up, but she held the pose. The unnamed woman broke her eye contact, and Emily's eyes shot open. Even from fifteen feet away, Massimo saw the fine filaments of red shot through her whites. She gasped and tipped over, breaking her pose but catching herself before she collapsed completely. She shook her head like she had water in her ear, shot a glare at the new woman, then crossed her legs in front of her, and stared off into the distance.

The rest of the students continued their warm-ups. Massimo ensured they kept good form in their core exercises, and by the time his view returned to Emily and the new woman, the new woman held the same boat pose that Emily had originally held, and Emily still sat cross-legged, eyes blank.

Massimo wandered closer to the pair. "Everything okay?" he whispered.

The nameless woman nodded, and Emily moved only her eyes to look at Massimo. Her mouth twitched, like she wanted to say something, but she remained silent.

Massimo returned to the front of the class. The rest of the first day involved simple leans against imaginary walls, or tabletops, or lampposts. None of the students were convincing, yet, except for the unnamed woman.

As they filed out of the warehouse, everybody said a quick goodbye but Emily, who gave barely a nod. The last person out was the new woman.

"Excuse me, I never got your name," said Massimo.

"Emily," she said as she walked out the door.

A Mime Is a Terrible Thing to Waste

"It was the weirdest god-damned thing, Alessandra," said Massimo, sitting across from his sister at Tsuji's.

"Weirder than a grown-ass man painting his face and not talking?" Alessandra said with a smirk. She was such a brat growing up. Always got her own way, but complained anyway. She talked early, he talked late. She got all the good genes that had skipped over him. But somehow he couldn't hold it against her.

She was an actress now, in small but growing parts. Massimo had no doubt she'd make it big one day. She'd gotten the performing gene too.

"That's our parents talking," he said.

"They can't believe you still do this."

Massimo bit into a tuna roll to avoid answering.

"So what, Emily is a super-common name," said Alessandra. "I went to school with like twelve Emilys. I could shout 'Emily' in this restaurant and I bet half of the girls here would perk up their heads."

"Please don't."

Alessandra smiled, a look that told Massimo she wouldn't—but only because she decided not to, not because he asked it of her.

"They don't understand why you have to constantly remind yourself of the past," said Alessandra.

"They don't have to."

"I don't understand, either."

Massimo clamped his mouth closed.

Alessandra continued. "You spent so much of your life not talking, why do you not talk for a living now? I would've thought you'd want to talk as much as possible, get it all out. Be a politician or a stand-up comedian or something."

"You'd have thought wrong."

"Clearly." Alessandra laughed, a crystalline sound that made Massimo feel happy to his core, no matter how annoying she was being at the moment. His enmity melted away.

"You talk enough for us both," said Massimo.

Alessandra shrugged in assent and pushed a lone piece of fish around on her plate with her chopsticks. "So what do you think is going on?"

"Nothing, really. This Emily—quiet Emily, well, I guess New Emily— she gives me the creeps. But it won't be the first time I've been weirded out by a student. The arts, you know. Attracts all kinds."

"You're not exactly normal yourself. You should at least perform, with all this practice."

"I'm fine teaching."

"You're not."

"I'll make a deal with you: I'll perform in public when you get your first speaking part."

"Don't make promises you can't keep." Alessandra popped the last piece of fish in her mouth.

Original Emily was a no-show the next class, but New Emily joined the group again. She still hadn't shown up on Massimo's roster. While his students stretched, he debated whether to toss her out. She didn't have a right to be there, and besides, she hadn't paid.

She looked up out of her stretch right as the thought of ejecting her crossed his mind. She smiled, all sweetness, but the expression didn't match her eyes. Massimo's skin became clammy, and he broke eye contact. He'd focus his energies on the other students. The paying ones. Then he wouldn't have to make a scene. After class, he'd politely ask

New Emily to register and pay or not return. Or maybe he wouldn't give her the first option.

"Facial expressions today," said Massimo.

New Emily contorted her face, and for a moment looked like the previous Emily, but then was back to herself. For the first time, Massimo realized how nondescript she was, and when he blinked, he immediately didn't remember what she looked like. Except she looked like old Emily. More and more. Or not. Massimo blinked hard, trying to clear his head.

The class applauded. They'd thought he was demonstrating a technique.

Emily had staked out a position next to Zeke. Zeke with cheeks of bubblegum. As Massimo demonstrated the oversized emotions necessary to carry a silent performance, Zeke's mimicking of his expressions was the best of all the students.

Toward the end of the class, Emily tapped Zeke on the shoulder and locked eyes with him. Massimo ignored the whole thing—he'd been relatively successful not looking at the strange woman during the class, he wasn't going to start now—and he concentrated on helping the others out with their cheek-busting smiles or eye-straining looks of surprise. When he glanced back at Zeke and Emily, Zeke's face had gone slack, the life drained from it. He'd turned from rubber to clay.

And she—well, she had the liveliest expressions.

"Zeke," said Massimo, but the man barely moved his head in reaction. Massimo turned back to the class and said, "Enough for today. Next week is pratfalls, so bring a cushion."

As the students filed out, Massimo stopped Zeke, who stared at him blankly and gave him a half nod and walked out.

"I'll see you next time," said New Emily, with Zeke's smile and Original

Emily's walk. Massimo remembered he was going to ask her to pay only after she'd left the building.

———

Massimo stood in the center of a city park, in full makeup, performing his routine, but something was very wrong, and he couldn't tell what. His sister, in a yellow dress, stood out in the crowd, and he tried to warn her of the danger, but he couldn't speak.

He woke up, sweating, and immediately yelled out loud to assure himself he could indeed talk.

He got his answer when a voice from the alley outside his window yelled, "Shut the fuck up, it's three in the morning."

———

"You look like shit," said Alessandra. They were shopping in the city. She needed a dress for an audition; he needed the company.

"Haven't been sleeping well," said Massimo.

"That girl still bothering you? I think you've got a crush." Alessandra stopped at a storefront and admired the stylish mannequins in the window of a vintage store.

Massimo shook his head. "I want nothing to do with her. I'm tossing her out next time she shows up."

"It's not that bad."

"It is that bad!" He sounded like a child, even to his own ears. The dreams had become more common—almost every night now—and he dreaded going to sleep. Always the same, giving a performance amidst a feeling of foreboding.

He hadn't had anxiety dreams about his delayed speech for years. He blamed New Emily.

"Your subconscious is telling you something," said Alessandra, heading into the store, Massimo in tow. "You should be out performing. Like me." She elongated the "me" into a beaming smile, her head tilted.

"I've been in a rut. I'm beginning to think you're right."

"That's the spirit. Maybe we should buy you something here as well!" Alessandra rummaged through a set of dresses on a clearance rack.

Massimo shook his head. "Don't get ahead of yourself."

Alessandra had that look in her eyes, the one that said she found something she had to have, and nothing was going to stand in her way. With a flourish, she whipped a vintage sundress off the rack: a pale lemon number.

"No," said Massimo, "not that one."

Alessandra laughed, "Silly brother, why do you care? This one is cute. It's totally me."

"Please listen to me, just this once."

"So serious." Alessandra widened her eyes and pushed her lips into a pout. She flung the dress over her arm and made her way to the counter to pay.

Massimo sighed, for the dress was the very same one she wore in all his dreams.

———————

The cancellations came in slowly. And they each said the same thing: the young woman Emily made them uncomfortable, and they felt the studio was no longer a safe space for them to learn the craft.

At least it's not just me, thought Massimo.

But that left him with no class to teach. He'd pleaded with the students, explaining that he'd take care of her the next time she showed up, and imploring them to come back. He hoped his appeals had changed some minds.

He was first into the warehouse that afternoon, and the giant space seemed even emptier than usual. It wasn't out of the ordinary for Massimo to get to the class before all his students, but he felt in the pit of his stomach that they weren't coming this time, despite his responses to their concerns.

Start time for the class arrived; no one came. Massimo waited. The air conditioner hummed as usual, but the air was getting warm, and Massimo felt flushed. Who was this mystery woman, who stole one person's physical essence and the other's face? Massimo still had no clue to her identity other than her first name—if that was her name at all.

Massimo admitted defeat. He might as well cancel the rest of the classes, as there was little reason to suspect his students would return. He was packing up his belongings when he heard the door swing open at the end of the warehouse.

In walked Emily.

There was something in the way she moved that nauseated Massimo. She wore a smile so devious, and her eyes were dark, almost black.

"Just you and me today," she said.

"What are you?"

She threw Zeke's grin at him, not breaking eye contact.

He felt his throat dry out. She tilted her head back and fluttered her eyelids languidly; he tried to yell at her, but his throat was filled with sand, and he needed a drink. He reached for his water bottle, and she held her palms to the ceiling. The water quenched his thirst, and moistened his throat, but he found he still couldn't speak.

"What are you doing to me?" he wanted to say, and did, in his head, but only a creak escaped his lips. No matter how hard he concentrated, he produced no words aloud.

And Massimo was five again, a little boy who wanted nothing more than to tell his family he loved them, or ask for an apple, or tell them where he hurt, but could not, and he was an elastic band ready to snap—the taunts from his classmates, the fistfights, the excruciating trips to the speech therapist, the medical procedure, all of it flooded back, and with every last bit of energy, he was able to expel a single word before he passed out: "No."

Massimo stood in the center of a growing crowd, in the middle of the city park. He didn't remember how he'd gotten there, but he knew he was supposed to be performing. He wore a three-piece suit, and the grease makeup weighed heavily on his face, causing him to sweat even more in the hot sun.

It made no sense: he wasn't a performer.

But here he was, performing the routine as he'd run through it in his mind so many times (wait—when did he run it through his mind?). This particular piece was a cross between traditional mime and silent statue, where he started out as the statue, making micro-movements, and didn't come alive until enough people developed a suspicion that perhaps he was not made of brass. He scanned the crowd as surreptitiously as he could, looking for clues to how he got there, or what or why he was performing. Nothing. Except a woman in a bright yellow dress, smiling. Alessandra.

Had she put him up to this? And had he repressed the preparation out of sheer nerves, only coming conscious when the performance was at hand? The crowd egged him on, and he felt like he was being watched by something malevolent. His head swam, and maybe he would faint.

His sister was in trouble, but he didn't know what threatened her. Fuzzy dark gray edges moved in on his vision. He fought through it, all the while performing—the show must go on—and he pushed the frayed edges of his vision back.

Emily stood next to his sister, smiling.

Oh god, no.

She moved closer to Alessandra.

No, not her.

"Take me," he thought.

"Take me," he wanted to say, but he couldn't.

"Take me," he tried to say, but no sound came from his mouth.

Emily gave him a look that said she'd already taken him, and he had nothing left to offer her.

The crowd murmured at his skill, but he didn't give a damn; only saving his sister mattered. He threw himself toward Emily, but he found himself unable to progress. "An invisible box!" squeaked a child. Massimo grunted as he failed to fight through the force holding him back.

Emily laughed as Massimo watched Alessandra's face slacken, and he tried to scream but he was drowned out by the crowd, even though he was making no noise, and he remembered this was a dream, but he somehow knew that this time, there was nothing to wake up from.

Christopher Degni writes about the magic and the horror that lurk just under the surface of everyday life. In his spare time, he works as a manager at an internet company in Cambridge, MA. He lives south of Boston with his wife (and his demons, though we don't talk about those). He's a graduate of the Odyssey Writing Workshop. This is his first fiction publication. You can contact him at the.writer.ced@gmail.com.

You Don't Choose the Circus Life, the Circus Life Chooses You

Lee Glenwright

"I've always had dreams about running away with the circus. I always have ever since I was young, going way back as far as I can remember." Varley's eyes held the brightest of gleams as he spoke, an almost lightning spark that was immediately at odds with his features, lined and shadowed as they were with the trappings of middle-age, of dreams that had been been allowed to go to waste, to almost spoil with resignation. "The smell of the greasepaint, the clamour and roar of the audience crammed inside the Big Top, the sugar-sharp tang of cotton candy as it melts away to a sweet hint of nothing on the tip of your tongue."

Zester—not his real name—smiled. Perhaps it could have been a grimace, the caked-on layers of white and red, in their gaudy contrast, making it hard to really be sure of the difference.

"I've seen you hanging around here on many a night," he said, "and I've wondered why it was that you always chose to stay back long after the shows were done and all of the props packed away ready for the next show." The thick, pale foundation had begun to crack in lines that matched the creases of the clown's eyes, flecks of second skin, lifting away

101

and threatening to somehow dilute the illusion. "The circus isn't the kind of life for everyone. Show after show, night after night. Always wearing a face to hide your own, it can stretch on for ever. And it's hard work. Make no mistake, it's hard."

Varley was undeterred. "Some children love horses, or running around the park in the summer evenings, shouting *tag* at one another. They seek to make their childhood stretch out forever, but they soon grow out of it as the realities of life, money, career, all take over. They always do in the end. This love of the circus and everything connected with it has always been *my* love, a pure, undiluted passion that has stayed with me, both as a child and into my adulthood." Perhaps it was the muffled sound of rehearsals drifting from inside the Big Top, or the bathing warmth of the sunshine in which he and the clown sat out back of the canvas tent, with its gaudy stripes of each and every colour he could think of and several more that he hadn't. The circus had arrived in town, bringing with it its cavalcade of wagons, fluttering banners and multi-coloured streamers, and the time for his dreams to come alive was *now.*

"Oh, I'm not trying to scare you or put you off, believe me," Zester said, the impossibly large crescent of red framing his mouth as he spoke. "Everyone would just love you to be a part of our big, happy family. The more the merrier. It's just that this circus life of ours is for *ever.*" Zester's face turned as serious as his drawn-on mask would allow. "It isn't just a job, something that you can walk away from at the end of a day. It's much more than that, it's your whole *life.* You understand that, don't you? It's true what they say. You don't just choose the circus life, the circus life chooses you. But once it has chosen you, you can't escape it."

"Escape it? Why would I ever want to do *that*? There's nothing that could possibly stop me. No reason holding me back. I've no family to consider, no true love to pine for," Varley said, the spark in his eyes, now ignited, refusing to dim. "I gave up on any of that a long time ago. More than anything, I want to be a clown. Oh yes, a *clown*! With my painted face and my bright, patchwork suit. Hearing the mirth, bathing in the laughter and adulation night after night, knowing that people *love* me for what I truly am. Knowing that I am bringing fun and enjoyment to the lives of others. Yes, I so want to be a clown!"

Zester rolled his eyes and made a smacking sound with his lips in a typical exaggerated gesture, as if weighing up what he had just heard. For just a moment, he looked almost serious behind his false visage. Varley felt his heart skip several beats.

"Very well then, if that's really what you want, if you're really, really certain, then a clown you shall be!" Zester said as he rolled his eyes again, his smile returning even broader than before. "As I said, the choice is really neither yours or mine to make, but one that was decided for you a long, long time ago. You have been chosen. Now, you should go home and have your very last night of freedom. Tomorrow, the Big Man will see you, the contracts will all be signed and then you will be one of us. Part of our big happy family!" He laughed, the sound raw and hearty, as the laugh of a clown should be, as Varley had always imagined it to sound.

"*Thank you! Oh, thank you!*" Varley cried, unable to believe quite what he was hearing, after so many years of daring to dream, of pushing everything else aside in favour of his one true passion. He got up to his feet, an imprint in the long grass where he'd been sitting, a dewy dampness clinging to the seat of his trousers going unnoticed.

He skipped home lighter than the air itself, each long step sloughing another year away from him, like layers of old skin being shed, fluttering away on the breeze. He felt himself being transported back to his childhood. To a Technicolor world of cotton candy and chocolate bars, of grazed knees and ointment and youth, drunk on the sights and sounds of the Big Top and all of the wonders that it had to offer.

He slept deep and well that night, the smell of fresh cut straw and sickly sweet popcorn filling his senses like the scent of a lost childhood, just waiting to be reclaimed.

The next day he had an eagerness about him that he couldn't recall ever experiencing. There was a light feeling in his belly and a trembling in his legs as he met The Big Man, sat in his dark office, tucked just behind the Big Top tent. Joy threatened to engulf him, a giddy feeling swallowing him up as agreements were spoken and contracts were made. The Big Man was happy, Varley would join the circus immediately, the newest member of its clown family. Now would start the rest of his life. Zester clapped him on the shoulder with a broad, gloved hand that almost sent him sprawling face first into the fresh, pine-scented sawdust.

"There you go. You're one of us now, a part of the family. Varley, that's a fine name for a clown, perhaps the finest name for a clown that there ever was. Varley the Clown!"

"*Varley the Clown*," he repeated, the words falling away from his tongue, the most normal, most right words that had ever been spoken or heard by anyone.

"But come, there's no time to dwell. There's so much work to be done, lots of work. Rehearsals! Costume! Make up!" Zester took him by the hand. "Come and meet the others. You'll be spending your life with them from here on in." With these words, Varley was introduced to everyone. The clown family, in their oversized shoes and their garish suits, the Strongman, with his bald, almost polished head gleaming under the hot lights and his clipped, waxy moustache that looked far too neat to possibly be real. He met Mister Energo, the magician, with his assistant, all long, tanned legs, sequins and feather boas of every colour he could imagine and more besides. Last but not least, he was introduced to the animal menagerie. Blaring elephants, prowling lions and horses, snorting and stamping in a cacophony that was the sweetest of music to his ears, a symphony that had filled his dreams on many a night, for as long as he could remember.

Home, Varley thought, his chest swelling with pride until it felt as if it could burst, *I'm home.*

It was show time.

The two hours that followed went by in a whirl of sights and sounds, the likes of which Varley had never dared to dream. The crowd bellowed out their appreciation as, one by one, the acts played out for their attention. They gasped as Mister Energo held light bulbs that glowed into incandescent life in his bare hands. They were awestruck as the lions were released, transforming the circus ring into some ancient arena as they snarled and stalked in all of their majesty. Last of all, they roared with laughter as the clowns fell about in a painstakingly choreographed chaos, pelting one another with foam pies. But most of all they reserved their love for Varley, the newest member of the circus show, born to be a clown. Ready to burst, he faced the blur of the audience, a huge smile of pride to complement the one painted across his face from ear to ear.

"That was a great show tonight," said Zeppo, another one of the clown troupe, with a genial slap to Varley's back as he did so. "They loved you, each and every one of them."

"Thanks," Varley said, his heart pounding, a sheen of sweat causing pockmark breaks in the thick greasepaint across his forehead. "I loved every minute. I could certainly get used to this way of life."

"Well, you've got plenty of time to do so," Zeppo said with a laugh, "*plenty.*" They both laughed, the sound echoing deep and hearty around the rear of the tent.

"So anyway, what did you do to end up here?" Zeppo asked.

"Oh, you know. It's just one of those things," Varley narrowed his eyes in thought as he tried to wipe makeup away from his face without much success, the thick greasy layer resisting the effort. "Childhood fantasy, you understand, surely."

Zeppo laughed again, the sound drawing the interest of the clowns sitting across from them. They seemed to look up as one. fixing their gaze in Varley's direction.

"No, that's not what I meant. What did you actually *do*, to wind up down here? Or can't you remember? That happens sometimes, it can take a little while."

Varley looked confused. "Down here? A little while?"

"Yeah, you know," Zeppo pointed a finger of his oversized glove at Zester, sitting with Gargantua, the Strongman. "Zester over there. He killed his wife and two children. Gargantua was a rapist. He lost count of his victims after they got into double figures, or so they say. Vicious brute of a man, he was. Pure evil."

"Killed...a *rapist?*" Varley almost whispered the words in confused disbelief, his mind whirling.

"Yeah, he got the chair once they caught up with him. As for me,

I was an arsonist. I burned a care shelter clean down to the ground. Killed sixteen folks, seven of them kids. Sometimes it feels like it was only yesterday. Anyway, it's pointless having regrets now. It was worth it at the time. I've always *loved* seeing things burn." He chuckled again. "Life's too short, isn't that what they all say? Except that it isn't, not really. So, what *is* your story?"

Varley wanted to talk, but no words would come. He could only stare, numb vines radiating out from his belly, spreading their icy chill to his heart. He scrubbed at the greasepaint again, harder now, rubbing at it with the palm of his hand. Still it refused to come away, stubborn. It must have been a joke. A dark joke, like some strange initiation. Except the looks on the faces of everyone around him said otherwise.

"You really haven't figured it out yet, have you? Oh well, like I said, you've got an eternity to remember. I'm sure it'll come back to you sooner or later. It usually does."

Varley felt sick, his stomach light, as though stuffed with too much sickly cotton candy. He looked at the other clowns, the strongman, the magician, all had risen to their feet and moved in towards him. His senses were flooded. The odour of cut straw and manure masking the heady, cloying stink of brimstone. The still-echoing laughter of the crowd barely hiding the wails of souls, naked screams of pain and torment destined to carry on forever. He looked at them as they encircled him, their eyes mocking him and their fingers pointing. Their faces stretched and distorted, shadows lengthening and coalescing, bleeding into one another like ghosts as they whirled around him ever faster in a spinning kaleidoscope of colours, their laughter becoming banshee wails of torment.

An eternity to figure it out. An eternity to remember.

"You know where you are and why you're here. You can go on telling yourself otherwise if it makes things easier."

You Don't Choose the Circus Life, the Circus Life Chooses You

He *did* remember. He remembered everything that he had kept hidden away, that he had done, that he had sought to bury away in life, never thinking that it would finally find him out. He thought of the Big Man, sat in his dark, dark office, bellowing out a deep, booming laugh that echoed on forever. He thought of the contract he'd signed, not in blood, but near enough.

He thought of all these things and he knew where he was. Exactly where he was and why he was there.

And when he said it aloud at last, wailing and crying in endless despair, not one of those other damned souls in that tent disagreed with him.

Lee Glenwright is a writer of dark fiction based in Sunderland, UK, where he lives with his family, a menagerie of reptiles, and a dark sense of humour. His work has appeared in a number of magazines and anthologies, including *Forever Hungry, Mrs Rochester's Attic,* and *Lovecraftiana Magazine.*

The Gleewoman of Preservation

Samantha Bryant

"CREEPY CLOWN HAUNTS LOCAL PLAYGROUND." The headline screamed across the page in twenty point gothic font. Maggie snorted. *This codswallop was news?* Honestly! Across the breakfast table, her husband looked up from his phone. "What?"

Maggie turned her newspaper so he could view the lurid headline. "A little over the top, don't you think?"

Her husband reached for the paper and she let him take it, picking up her coffee and taking a sip. It was still a little too hot and burned her upper lip. She touched the sore place with her fingertip. Not too bad. It probably wouldn't even redden that much. George always did make the coffee superheated. She joked it was because his heart was just that cold. This is what it took to defrost him.

He was back on his phone now, apparently in an active chat. She sighed, wondering why she bothered to get out of bed to have breakfast with him anymore. It wasn't like they talked. They might as well be two strangers on the bus. Maybe it would be better when he retired too here in a couple more years. Maybe it would be worse. Time would tell.

Suddenly, George stood. "I'm going to have to go," he said, shoving his arms through his suit-jacket sleeves. He knocked his phone onto the floor.

Maggie glanced at the clock as she moved to pick it up for him. It was still only six-thirty. "So early?"

George took a gulp from his still steaming mug, unfazed by the tongue-searing heat. "Things are already on fire over there."

Maggie held out the phone, startled to see a group chat labeled "Gleemen." The last message said, "EMERGENCY. Here. Now." *What was the man up to?*

George pocketed the device, leaned over and gave her kiss on the cheek, lips still warm from the coffee. "Lunch today?"

Maggie nodded, pulling her bathrobe tight around her.

As soon as George was out of the house, Maggie went to the bedroom and pulled on her retirement uniform of yoga pants and a voluminous blouse, ran a comb through her gray and brown mop of hair, and grabbed her purse. *What in the world were Gleemen?*

Crackpot theories went through her head. She'd heard stories about women her age finding out they'd been living a lie all these years, that their husbands have secret lives they've known nothing about. Mistresses. Gay lovers. Shady business ventures. Dark hobbies. She had to know what George was doing. It was the surest way to shut down her hyperactive imagination.

She pulled out her phone and used the location service to ping George's. He was at the Shriners club, just over on the other side of the river. *Was the emergency just an early morning drink with his buddies?* She put the car in drive and went to investigate.

A few minutes later, she was parked two blocks from the clubhouse, at Cup-a-Joe. She was a regular at the coffee shop, so no one would think anything of her car sitting in the lot, not even her husband, if he spotted it.

Locking the car, she took the path through the alley into the small patch of trees that bordered the clubhouse. It had been the VFW building before that organization raised the funds to build something more elaborate and the Shriners took over the old watering hole. This clubhouse was more like a shack, a simple two-room building, with weathered cedar shake siding and a drooping front stoop. It was one of the oldest structures left in town. Not that it made any difference to its value. The place was an awkward eyesore. The hand-lettered sign was faded to near illegibility, the crescent and scimitar looking more like a wonky eye with a weird inverted eyebrow now.

But clearly, something was going on in there. Eight cars were crammed into the tiny parking area, including George's. She recognized four of the other vehicles as belonging to other men she knew from Shriners' events. As she stood watching, another car came too quickly down the road and slid to a stop in the gravel parking lot, raising a plume of white smoke that settled into dust on the shiny blue metal. The driver left the car where it had landed, blocking in the others. He leaped from the seat and scurried into the building, arms full of a large lumpy bundle inside a garbage bag.

Maggie steadied herself with a hand on a tree trunk as she leaned out to watch the man enter the building. It had to be Mr. Maxwell, the one they all called "Doc" even though he had retired twenty years ago. There was no mistaking his mad scientist hair, but she'd never seen him move like that. He wasn't even limping. He moved like a man half his eighty years, even with that unwieldy bundle in his arms.

Curiosity stoked like a blazing fire, Maggie left her hiding place to approach the back of the clubhouse, where she knew the men would be gathered around the table in the back room. The window was too high to

111

see into, but some of the men talked loud enough to be heard through the walls and the cracked window frame. She got there right as Doc entered the room and heard the other men calling out to him.

She sat on the wooden box that held yard tools, testing its sturdiness warily. She'd probably gets chips of old paint stuck to her pants, but it was better than standing while she eavesdropped. The box groaned only a little as it took her weight. It probably creaked less than her knees would have. Inside the clubhouse, she heard a lot of rattling plastic and exclamations that didn't make much sense to her. "I'll take the stripes." "Green or purple?" "Who's got the three o'clock today?"

Finally, she couldn't take it anymore. She had to see. She clambered up to stand on the box, putting her head at level with the bottom of the window and giving her a limited view of the room. About a dozen men gathered around the table. Maggie was surprised to spot a couple of younger men from around town alongside the familiar old men of the Shriners Club.

She spotted Henry Carver, who had occupied the middle seat in her social studies classroom not too many years ago and Doc's grandson, the third generation of doctors to work out of the pediatrician's practice on King Street. Doc's grandson was talking. "And if this doesn't work?"

Maggie's own husband answered from where he stood, examining some kind of chart on the far wall. "Then, we'll try something else. But if we can starve it out, it'll go dormant for another thirty years. All we have to do is make sure that no one gets near The Pit until then."

The Pit? Now that was interesting. "The Pit" was what everyone called the remnants of the original townsite. A collection of crumbling stone chimneys and a few other pieces of the original buildings that hadn't completely rotted away over the centuries sloped down into a wide crater. The local story was that the founding fathers had built on some kind of sinkhole without knowing it and one spring afternoon, the entirety of the town had simply fallen into the earth, killing nearly everyone. The few survivors had rebuilt nearby, and the old townsite remained a local curiosity, the hatchery for ghost and monster stories for generations, and the occasional site of additional tragedies, usually involving young people, alcohol, and dares.

It made sense to keep people away from The Pit as much as possible. In fact, Maggie had been part of a movement by the women in the town, back when she was young, to try and get the city to put up barriers of some sort to keep people out. Despite the deaths of two young men that soggy spring, the town had only opted to put up more warning signs and add an additional patrol by the police each night. Maybe they'd been right. It had been years since anyone had been stupid enough to venture out there and get themselves hurt or killed. In fact, it had been almost exactly thirty years since those last tragedies.

While she'd been woolgathering, the men had begun to gather their belongings. Maggie scrambled down off the box and squatted awkwardly in the rhododendron bushes that grew against the side of the building. She'd end up with spiders in her hair, but if she was quiet, she could probably avoid being noticed as the men left. The thought of the Shriners finding her spying on them was embarrassing enough to keep her hiding there for a good ten minutes after she'd stopped hearing car doors slam and tires moving over gravel.

After she stood up and dusted off her clothes, she walked up onto the back deck, and pressed her face against the dingy glass to peer into the room where the men had been meeting. The lights were off now, so she couldn't make out much beyond the shadows of pieces of furniture. She tried the doorknob, and, to her surprise, it turned easily in her hand. After a quick look around to be sure she was unobserved, she let herself into the building.

The Gleewoman of Preservation

She'd been in the room before, of course, during picnics and family days, but it seemed a different space while the sun was still rising on a sleeping town and she stood there alone. The dim sunlight filtered through the dirty windows seemed to highlight rather than dissipate the shadows. Brushing off her irrational foreboding feeling, Maggie walked to the wall where her husband had been standing a few minutes earlier. The chart he'd been looking at was complicated, with rings of different colors intersecting. She thought she recognized some astrological signs alongside less familiar symbols. She couldn't make much sense of it. Pulling out her phone, she snapped a photo of it so she could examine it at her leisure later. Then, she made for the exit.

She paused at her car and looked into the side view mirror before she went into the coffee shop. It was a good thing she'd stopped to check. There were sticks in her hair and a bit of dewy web attached to her sweater. After putting herself into better order, she grabbed her purse and walked into Cup-a-Joe.

Waving at the barista, another former student, she went to her favored table in the back corner. No need to order; they knew what she liked here. The high narrow table was too tall for most customers, so it was nearly always empty. Maggie's unusual height meant she was uncomfortable in most public seating, so she appreciated the proportions of this table and chair, as well as the view it afforded of the rest of the room. Prime people watching.

Suzanne brought her drink and plain bagel with cream cheese, setting both down wordlessly before heading back to her station behind the bar. Maggie sipped her coffee as she thought about what she'd seen and what it might mean. In the half-hour or so that she sat there, the shop filled in with other townies who didn't have to be somewhere else by nine a.m., local business owners, students, and retirees. She knew most of the customers by sight and a lot of them by name. They knew her, too, of course, which was why they waved in greeting but didn't come over to chat. They knew she liked quiet with her coffee, not conversation.

That wasn't exactly true. What she liked was other people's conversation. Maybe it was a habit she had picked up in years of teaching, this listening in as a way to find out what was going on. Maybe she was just a natural busybody. But either way, listening to the coffee shop talk in the morning gave her pulse of the town and there was little she didn't know about. That was probably why her husband's mysterious behavior irked her so. It didn't seem right that the biggest mystery in her life right now was the man who sat across from her at breakfast.

She pulled out her phone and clicked on the photo of the weird chart, zooming in on different parts of it for a closer look as she nibbled at her bagel. Twenty minutes into her breakfast, Suzanne showed up with a fresh cup and picked up the money Maggie had left on the table. She was good people, that one. Maggie hoped that the new boyfriend was going to turn out to be worthy of her. She deserved better than the last one had turned out to be.

Maggie was just considering heading for home to take a shower before her lunch date with her husband, when the two young men she'd seen at the Shriners came in. They weren't regulars at this shop, so they walked over to the coffee bar and talked with Suzanne for a few minutes, making their choices before they sought a table. Maggie was pleased when they chose the one just to her left. She turned to her right, seeming to be looking out the window, but really, she was watching their reflection in the glass.

Doc's grandson looked agitated. Henry Carver seemed more thoughtful. He leaned back in his chair and looked over the room. His gaze lingered for a moment in her direction–probably he recognized her, but he didn't say anything. He smiled when Suzanne brought the coffee drinks and wrapped his hands around the warm mug breathing in the steam before he picked it up for a drink.

"You think they're right?" Doc's grandson asked, seeming to pick up a conversation that had already been in progress.

"They've done this before."

The young Mr. Maxwell leaned in, his suit jacket bunching up behind his neck. "Yeah. But last time, two people died."

Maggie picked up her empty cup, pretending to drink out of it. This she wanted to hear.

"Yeah. Only two. We got off easy. Remember what they said about sixty years ago?"

Young Doc Maxwell nodded. "But this plan. Can it really be that simple? It seems...well, it seems kind of ridiculous."

Henry shrugged. "I hope it works. Because I don't like the sound of the alternatives."

The two men sat for a while in silence, sipping their coffees. Maggie still held her empty cup, hoping for more details. When it seemed like the conversation had well and truly ended, she gathered up her purse and jacket. As she turned to leave, she pretended she had only just spotted Henry. "Henry Carver? Is that you?"

He stood. "Hello Mrs. Dudley! How are you?"

"You can call me Maggie now, you know. We're both adults."

Henry looked at his shoes, just as he had done when he was fifteen years old and embarrassed to admit he hadn't done his homework. "No ma'am, I don't think I can do that." They both laughed. He gestured at his companion. "Do you know Jim?"

"I don't know that we've met." Maggie offered the other man her hand to shake. "But I know your grandfather I think. Isn't he a Shriner, too?"

Young Doc Maxwell looked surprised and Henry jumped in. "Her husband is George Dudley. I'm sure you've met him."

"Oh yes. Fine fellow. My grandfather speaks highly of him."

"I'd better be going, but it was so nice to see you Henry, and nice to meet you, Jim." Both young men mumbled their goodbyes and settled back into their chairs behind her. Maggie went back to her car, wheels spinning in her brain. What had happened sixty years ago? That would have been when Maggie was a little girl, still living in Virginia with her parents. She had never heard of Preservation, North Carolina until she accepted the English literature position at the high school when she was nearly thirty years old. She didn't remember anyone talking about a town tragedy, but maybe the intervening years had been enough to move the incident out of common gossip.

Checking her phone, Maggie decided she had time for a visit to the library before she headed home to change for lunch.

The reference librarian was happy to set Maggie up in the local history room. The dust on the tabletops attested to how little use the room saw. That was a shame. If there was any history that might engage young people, it would be the local stuff. But young people were always looking ahead, and hadn't yet learned that you could also learn by looking back. So often, by the time we take an interest in the past, the people who could have told us what happened have passed on. But, that is why we have books.

Maggie flipped through a couple of books that purported to be histories of the town of Preservation, but amounted to little more than surface glosses with more pictures than words and nothing of any interest. One of them didn't even mention The Pit or the sinkhole that destroyed the original settlement back in the 1619. Surely, that was a moment to warrant mention in a history of the town.

The Gleewoman of Preservation

The story Maggie knew about the naming of the town claimed that the original settlers, who were rumored to be survivors of the lost colony of Roanoke, arrived in the late 1500s and in gratitude for finding a safe haven, named the place Preservation. No official records exist of that time, and the books that did talk about the town's founding were forced to use words like "rumor" and "legend" when details were hazarded.

The first real records of the town picked up in 1609, a scant ten years before the fledgling settlement was swallowed by the earth. They were dull reading, mostly made up of lists kept by an industrious farmwife who tracked her family's resources with great zeal.

Getting herself back on task, she looked for more recent history. Sixty years ago, the boys had said. 1959. If there'd been some kind of tragedy, you'd think it would be in one of the books, but it wasn't. Summoning the reference librarian again, Maggie got set up with a microfiche reader and a little box of yellowish plastic cards. She scanned through quickly, checking only the main headline and the obituaries of each issue of the paper in 1959. She read about a beauty queen who'd made a good showing in a statewide competition, a politician who had shamed himself with public drunkenness, and a controversy at the school about the hiring of a black teacher. Ordinary small town news. Nothing detailing deaths.

When she reached into the box for the next card, she found it was missing. No card for June, July, August, or September. The October card was headlined by the reopening of the high school after a kitchen fire had caused damage the month before. That was it. Maggie leaned back in her chair, considering. The dangerous part about hard-copy records like these is that information could be destroyed, lost, or stolen. She wondered which had happened to these microfiche cards.

She went through the motions of asking the reference librarian, but, as she expected, the librarian was bewildered, too. The woman couldn't find any notation saying the microfiche had been sent out on loan, but she dutifully promised to inquire amongst the rest of the staff and to contact Maggie when the materials were found.

As Maggie left, now in a hurry to get cleaned up before she met her husband for lunch, her heart was beating fast. This whole thing just kept getting more and more mysterious. What happened sixty years ago? She couldn't have explained why she was so sure, but she was convinced the microfiche would never be found. She felt equally confident that any other records of the time would have been damaged or gone mysteriously missing as well.

She arrived at the usual diner on time, her hair was still wet and her mind still reeling. Her husband smiled as she entered, though, and stood up, an old fashioned gesture of respect that pleased her. She leaned in and kissed him on the cheek before she took her chair. "Running late today?" he asked, pointing at her damp curls.

"I lost track of time." True enough. She didn't have to tell him what she'd been doing that had her distracted. "Fire out?"

"Huh?" George looked confused.

"This morning? At work? You said things were already on fire over there."

"Oh. Yes, yes. It's all right now. We've got a plan in place."

"That's good." Maggie picked up the menu and started looking it over. Somehow she just didn't feel like having the same thing she always did today. "Have you ever tried the Sante Fe shrimp?"

George sputtered into his water glass. "What? No chicken today?"

"Just feeling like trying something new."

Her husband looked her up and down appraisingly, but didn't offer further comment. Maggie ate faster than usual, anxious to get back to her inquiries, but George surprised her by announcing that he was taking the afternoon off. "I'm a little under the weather. Think I'll take the afternoon off and take a nap."

She hoped he wasn't doing that to keep her company. Today of all days, she wasn't bored. "Oh okay."

"You don't sound thrilled to have me at home."

"It's not that." *It was totally that.* "I've just got my patterns here in my retirement. You know I've always liked my schedules and plans."

"I'll stay out of your way."

So, instead of sneaking into the Shriners clubhouse to look for more clues or hunting down octogenarians with loose lips at the senior center, Maggie was stuck at home that long afternoon, watching the occasional car drive down their street and sipping a cup of tea while her husband sawed logs in the bedroom. She wondered if he snored like that at night, too, and she was just so used to it after all these years that she didn't hear it anymore. It was like machinery in there. Relentless. Eventually, she decided she'd take a walk to get away from the noise.

When she opened the hall closet to pull out her sun hat, George's work bag fell over at her feet, spilling. She knelt to pack it back up, groaning a little as her knees cracked. She really needed to get some kind of exercise program going or she was going to spent her retirement too stiff to enjoy herself. Promising herself a session of yoga the next morning, she scooped up the spilled items: a legal pad covered in her husband's flowing handwriting, an empty travel mug, and his office keys as well as some pens and a chapstick. When she shoved the bag back into the closet, it pressed against a plastic bag filled with something soft.

Curious, Maggie pulled it out. It appeared to be a kitchen garbage bag full of clothes of some kind. Had George been doing a closet clean out without her? She loosened the drawstring to peek inside and was startled by a riot of color: stripes, polka-dots, and sequins. "What in the world?"

"It's a costume," George said, appearing behind her. "We're thinking of marching as clowns in the parade this year." He reached to take the bag from her and Maggie let him. He placed it back in the closet. "I'm supposed to try these on and see if they'll work for me."

"Clowns? Really? Do you think that's a good idea?"

"Sure, why not?"

"Well, a lot of people find them kind of creepy."

George shrugged. "We're the friendly kind."

"Won't you be too hot? I mean, some of you get all red faced just walking in your suit jackets and wearing the fezzes." Maggie had a vision of a bunch of middle-aged men sweating their way down the street, with white face paint melting onto their lapels. It wasn't pretty.

George looked thoughtful. "That's a good point. I'll mention it to the guys. We're not as young as we used to be, after all. Maybe it's not such a good idea."

That night's dinner was popcorn. In all her excitement that morning, Maggie had completely forgotten to make a dinner plan or go grocery shopping. The larder was bare. George took it well, and they agreed to turn it into a movie night. After the film ended, they sat there on the sofa in silence for a moment. Maggie took the popcorn bowl off her husband's lap and moved it the end table, then twisted on the sofa so she was facing him.

"What was it like here in Preservation when you were a kid?" George startled and Maggie was glad she'd moved the popcorn bowl before she'd asked. He'd have flung buttery kernels everywhere. Her suspicions were raised anew about that morning meeting at the Shriners, but she played it cool. "I was at Cup-a-Joe this morning and I heard someone talking about some deaths sixty years ago. You'd have been about six, I guess?"

George nodded. "I remember hearing something about it, but I was a kid, so I probably didn't get the whole story."

"What happened?"

Standing up, George shook a couple of stray puffs of popcorn off his pants. "If I remember right, it was a group of teenagers who'd snuck out into the woods to party." He crossed the room and stood looking out the window. "There was some kind of accident, I guess. A bunch of them died." He turned back around to face Maggie. "Our moms kept all of us on a short leash that whole summer. Mostly I just remember how boring it was being stuck at home all the time."

"So, you don't know what happened?" Maggie wasn't calling him on it yet, but she knew the man was lying. After thirty-five years of marriage, she knew all his tells. He knew she knew, too. That's why he was avoiding eye contact.

"Not really. Like I said, I was just a little kid at the time."

"Seems weird that I've never heard about it before. A town doesn't just get over the loss of a group of young people like that."

"Sometimes people don't like to talk about painful things."

Maggie got up and picked up the bowl to take to the kitchen. She felt George relax behind her. When she was almost out of the room, she turned around, as if she'd just remembered. "Where did it happen?"

"Huh?" George patted his pockets, probably looking for his phone.

She picked it up from the table by the door and brought it to him. "The accident. Where did it happen? You said, 'out in the woods,' but where?"

George kept his gaze on the phone. "I don't know." His voice was cold. He obviously wanted her to let this go. That realization only made her curiosity burn all the brighter.

"Was it out at The Pit?"

George dropped his phone. She watched him pick it up and saw his hand shaking a little. "I suppose it might have been," he said.

Maggie left George to his own devices until it was time to get ready for bed, bustling around the house and keeping herself busy while her mind spun theories about what her husband was up to and what he was trying to hide from her.

After they'd gone to bed, she lay awake for a while after George's breathing settled into the deeper rhythms of sleep, thinking and listening. She finally drifted off and spent a tumultuous night chasing imaginary children down dark alleys and hearing weird laughter in her dreams. She was only vaguely aware of it when her husband climbed back into bed toward dawn.

George was slow to get up the next morning. She was already at the table with some buttered toast and eggs on her plate when he stumbled into the kitchen bleary-eyed and grumpy. "You feeling okay?" His answer was more of a grunt than a string of words. "Maybe you should take a sick day, go back to bed for a while." He grunted again and she let it go. He was a grown man. She couldn't make him be reasonable if he was determined to be an idiot.

After a few more minutes fumbling, he joined her at the table, groaning as he dropped into the chair as if the motion was painful. Maggie peered at him over her mug of coffee, but he didn't look back at her. He picked up his cup, winced, and sloshed coffee across the table trying to set it back down. Maggie hopped up and grabbed a kitchen towel to mop up the mess before it spilled onto the floor.

Crisis averted, she turned to her husband. "You okay? Did you burn yourself?" She reached for his hand, but he pulled it in tight to his chest, cradling it. His pajama shirt sleeve slid up his forearm and Maggie saw a dark black mark almost like a thin tire skid on his skin. "George! Your arm!"

He stood up, stepping back so she couldn't reach him. "It's all right, Maggie. Just a bruise. It's no big deal."

"What would give you a bruise like that?"

George frowned, which made him look constipated. "I was helping move some file boxes and one fell on my arm. It hurts, but I've already had it checked out. It's fine. I didn't want to worry you."

A file box? Leaving a mark that looks like something had seared his skin? Did he really expect her to believe that load of hogwash? She stood there gaping like a fish, unable to even form words to express her mix of emotions. George turned away, tugging his sleeve down protectively over the injury. "You know what? I think I am going to take your advice and go back to bed. Can you call in for me?"

Still stunned into silence, Maggie nodded and stood there in the middle of the kitchen staring at the place where her husband had been standing for a long minute after he had gone. She crossed o the hall where they still kept an old-fashioned wall-mounted house phone and used it to call George's boss. The secretary sounded a little startled–George almost never missed work–but she agreed to pass on the message and Maggie hung up.

When she returned to sit at the table, she found that her knees felt wobbly beneath her and her hand shook when she freshened her cup. She picked up the newspaper, only slightly discolored along the bottom by the spilled coffee. The frontpage article showed a blurry photograph of a person standing at the edge of the woods, dressed as a clown. She pulled the paper close to her nose to peer at it.

The clown wore baggy striped pants and a polka-dot vest. Maggie drew in a sharp breath, remembering the clothing she'd found in the closet and George's unlikely parade story. She scanned the headline. MORE CLOWN SIGHTINGS AT EDGE PARK. Edge Park was right on the border of the woods on the east side of town, the woods that housed the sinkhole that had once been Preservation's first site. The selfsame woods where two teenage boys had been killed messing about at the Pit, back when she was a new bride, having found George when she'd begun to believe she might never marry. Those boys had been her students.

She scanned the article, but it didn't say much. Just quoted the children who had spotted the clown. "It didn't do anything. Just stood there. It was enough to scare me! I ran back home." Maggie remembered the two young men in the coffee shop and how they said the plan had seemed ridiculous, but they hoped it would work. What could be more ridiculous than dressing up like clowns to scare people away?

She glared at the picture. The man in the clown suit looked to be about six foot tall, broad in the shoulder and soft in the middle, though she supposed that could have been padding as part of the costume.

But the stance.

The way he leaned against the tree. Too familiar to be denied. That was her husband standing there. Maggie heard the paper flutter to the floor behind her as she sped to the bedroom. George had some explaining to do, sick or not, hurt or not, asleep or not.

She flung open the bedroom door so hard it bounced back and nearly hit her in the forehead. Shoving past it, she grabbed the blankets and pulled them back, only to reveal an empty bed. "George?" She leaned into the bathroom. *Empty.* "George!" She peered into the home office. *Dark. Empty.* In another two-minute whirlwind exploration, she'd discovered what her heart had known immediately. The man was gone. Snuck out, probably out the back door while she was on the phone.

The weird injury on her husband's arm flashed against her memory again. She'd only gotten a glimpse, but she'd known it wasn't an ordinary bruise. The wound was long and straight, like something had been wrapped around his arm. And that was him in the newspaper, dressed as a clown. Her husband was wrapped up in something all right. Something dark and dangerous. And she wasn't having it!

Maggie was dressed and standing at the door with her keys in hand in a matter of minutes. She froze there, realizing she had no idea where to go. She pulled out her phone and texted George. He obviously didn't want to tell her what he was up to, so she would investigate on her own. "Going to Edge Park to look for you. You've got some explaining to do."

An empty playground is a disturbing sight. Usually, even on a school day, you'd find some toddlers and their mothers or a teenager skipping school hanging out. But no one was at Edge Park. Maggie stood next to the old-fashioned merry-go-round that squeaked as it spun slowly in the light morning breeze. She checked her phone. No messages. No bars either. She put it away.

Swinging her purse around behind her, she marched toward the woods. As she neared the tree line, she swore the temperature dropped a good ten degrees. She buttoned her sweater as she walked and considered going back to her car for the coat she'd left in the back seat. She was afraid she'd lose her nerve if she stopped, so she kept moving. Her heart began to thump in her ears.

Once she crossed the tree line, the first thing she noticed was how wet everything seemed, like there had just been a heavy rain. It had been dry for more than a week, so that was strange enough, but stranger still was the smell. It reminded her of seaweed that had rotted on a beach, something fetid and salty, over-ripe and beginning to mold.

The next thing she noticed was the silence. No birdsong. No skittering of small animals. No breeze rustling the greenery. She began to perspire under her sweater even though she could now see her breath in the cold. She took a step backwards. This had been a bad idea. Another. She was on the verge of turning tail and running when something grabbed her ankle and tugged. She fell to the ground with a bruising thump. Looking down, she saw a strange mark on her ankle, where bare skin showed beneath the hem of her capri pants. A long slender black mark, that looked too much like the one she'd seen on her husband's arm.

She scuttled back toward the tree line on her butt, shaking too hard to regain her feet, but desperate to escape. This time she saw the thing that streaked out from the underbrush, a long black slender whip. It hit the ground next to her foot and she yelped, scooting backward again. She didn't see the second attack coming until the black tendril was wrapped around her calf, sending shooting pains up her leg. She screamed and pulled. Whatever gripped her snaked around her leg a second time, and even through her pants, she could feel a strange heat and a tight squeeze.

Scrambling, she swung her purse round to her belly and thrust her hand inside, coming away with a small pair of gardening shears she'd been meaning to return to one of her friends. She opened the blades and dove for her own knee, jabbing the point into the black thing. It rippled and she felt the squeeze on her calf. She opened the blades wider and cut through the whip. Suddenly free, she rolled onto her belly and clambered to her feet, careening toward the tree line in an awkward lurching run. Something wet ran down her leg but she didn't stop to examine it.

She made it through into the daylight and stumbled straight into Henry Carver. "Mrs. Dudley!" He sounded half-surprised and half-relieved. "Get behind me." He gave Maggie a non-too-gentle shove and she spun closer to the center of the park. Henry flipped a weird looking gun into shooting position and aimed it at the woods. "On my count!" he yelled. That's when Maggie noticed the other men who were all running towards the edge of the woods, all similarly armed.

She sat down on the ground, her knees giving way. Henry shouted again. "Three-two-one!" and all the men rushed the woods with their strange guns. It was only when she smelled the smoke and charred meat scent that she realized they'd all been carrying flame-throwers.

The park was a mess of activity for the next few minutes, but Maggie stayed where she was, letting it all flow around her. After a fire truck had been through, someone dropped down in the grass beside her. It was George. He pulled her into his shoulder in a rough hug and she let him. There was time to be angry later. Right now, she was just glad to be alive.

"What was that thing?" she asked.

"We call it Thurston."

"Thurston?"

George smiled. "Sure. Can't have ordinary folks overhearing us talking about monsters in the woods." She noticed that his injured arm was wrapped now. Probably Doc Maxwell, the older or the younger, had seen to it. "These days, someone would be wandering around in there with a camera, hoping to become a YouTube star and get themselves eaten. Better to make it sound like someone's grandfather. Old and boring."

Maggie looked down at her leg. Something black and slick still clung to her pants. A greenish ooze covered her calf and ankle, down to the black burn just above her sock.

Her husband grabbed her hand when she reached for it. "Doc Maxwell will want that. He's been after a sample to study."

"He can have it."

George waved, and someone came with a set of tongs and a plastic bag and unwrapped the tentacle from her calf. Maggie winced, but didn't cry out as it was pried loose. George helped her to her feet. "Come on. Let's get you over to Doc's place. We'll get you patched up and sworn in."

"Sworn in?"

"Oh yeah. You've done it now, you old busybody. You're a Gleeman now. Or a Gleewoman, I guess. No more blissful ignorance for you."

She glanced back at the woods. One of the men was standing there at the tree line again, wearing green pants with a pink polka-dotted shirt and a giant jacket, which she now realized probably hid a flamethrower.

She turned back to her husband. "That's for the best. You really need a better cover story if you want to keep people out of there. I mean, really, clowns?"

George shrugged. "People are afraid of clowns."

"Sure, sure." Maggie grimaced as George helped her into the passenger seat of her car. "But they're more frightened of flesh-eating viruses. Why not just claim the area is contaminated?"

George sat with his hands on the steering wheel, tilting his head thoughtfully. "I think I'm going to be glad you're with us. You've got a good head on your shoulders."

Maggie rested against the window as her husband drove them away, grateful her head was still there, where it belonged. She had a feeling she'd need her wits about her if she was going to survive retirement in Preservation, North Carolina.

Samantha Bryant teaches Spanish to middle schoolers, so mere clowns aren't enough to scare her. She writes *The Menopausal Superhero* series, and other feminist-leaning speculative fiction. When she's not writing or teaching, Samantha enjoys family time, watching old movies, baking, reading, gaming, walking in the woods with her rescue dog, and going places. Her favorite gift is tickets (to just about anything). You can find her on Twitter and Instagram @samanthabwriter or at samanthabryant.com

auguste

Charles R. Bernard

"Something's wrong with Gus," you tell Vinegar Vic. Vic grimaces, spits a wad of something foul at the rough wooden floorboards, and continues to fumble with the back of his costume. Its soft white silk is as radiant and slippery as a moonbeam. "Give me a hand with these fucking buttons," he snarls.

Backstage smells like old canvas, popcorn, frying dough, and the swamp-grass, weed-killer smoke of Vic's sherm-stick. Vic has been smoking sherms—tobacco and cannabis dipped in PCP, which Vic calls "embalming fluid"—for years. Decades, maybe, to look at his weathered face, the wrinkles and blown capillaries that the greasepaint hides so well. But he's only started pulling gags under the jagged influence in the last year or so. A bad sign, in your opinion. Trouble coming.

"The fuck is wrong with you?" he snaps, and you flinch and start to help with his suit. It's beautiful, pristine and as ghost-white as Vic's greasepaint, tight at the wrists and ankles but otherwise voluminous, with black pom-poms down the front. It cost a fortune, once upon a time, and even as Vic swills whisky from a brown glass pint bottle and hits his sherm, he spills neither a drop nor a fleck of ash onto it.

auguste

"I think he's sick," you tell Vic as you deftly button the suit. Your fingers are fleet and sure—they always have been, in contrast to your words, which have always formed slowly in your mind and fallen sluggishly off of your tongue. "He's been.... wrong. Since Minneapolis." Maybe Vic hears you over the boom and thump of the music on the loudspeakers. Maybe not—either way, he doesn't respond. The spotlight splashes sporadically through the gaps in the heavy stage curtain and scatters angular shadows, etching Vic in strobe-light bursts; white greasepaint, features carefully outlined in black, conical white silk hat over a bald cap. Over the reek of Vic's sherm and the liquor oozing out of his pores, you smell makeup, latex, and spirit gum, and, below that, the days-old cumin funk of Vic's unwashed body.

Vic's last drag on his smoke is a deep one, and the hiss and crackle is audible through a break in the music. Vic grinds the butt out on the paper plate by his elbow, and you wince. He's been asked not to smoke back here— the risk of fire—but nobody relishes a confrontation with him. The plate's surface is stained bright yellow and smeared with the remnants of four fried eggs with extra butter, Vic's hangover cure of choice. You'd brought him the eggs not an hour earlier. You'd passed Gus to bring them from the kitchen— well, passed the darkened alcove where Gus has been spending more and more of his time. Gus himself had not been visible, and you'd hurried onward after you'd hesitated and peered for a moment into the deep shadows and crooked, hanging canvas in the back of the tent. You'd wanted to check on Gus, but cowardice won out. You'd felt watched, and it hadn't been a feeling of being spied on by another person as much as it had been a feeling of hungry, alien regard; the eyes of a lion, perhaps. In fact, you'd even thought you'd smelled something for a moment—something big and predatory, with blood on its breath. But Circus Madrigal doesn't have lions anymore—hasn't had them for years. Too big a hassle, thanks to the animal rights people.

132

"AND NOW," boom the loudspeakers. Zorba the ringmaster, introducing Vinegar Vic's act. Vic's pupils are blown and his eyes are jitterbugging in his skull, but he doesn't miss his cue; out the curtain he goes, breaking into an exaggerated run as he does so. As the whiteface clown, it's Vic's job to start the act and warm things up with his Pierrot character. Mime work, maybe a little juggling if he's not too fucked up to find the prop table in the middle of the ring. Zorba brushes by you on his way offstage. His nostrils flare at the chemical-and-cannabis reek of Vic's sherm, and his black eyes immediately fix on the butt crushed onto the plate of egg remnants. The string of curses he mutters would blacken his moustache, if it were possible for its bristles to get any blacker.

"*Always* with this shit," he says to you. He's not angry at you, you know, but you happen to be nearby, which earns you a front-row seat to his anger. You are often in that position—you are, after all, often nearby, sweeping or carrying or fetching or, as in this case, helping Vinegar Vic into his costume. "*Always* with this fucking PCPs," Zorba continues, thrusting one blunt digit at the plate. In a fleeting splash of light from the ring, you can see smeared white greasepaint fingerprints on the edge of the offending butt where Vic gripped it.

"I think Gus is sick," you tell Zorba, slowly enunciating the words. Zorba's eyes move to your face and soften. "Sick?" he asks. Zorba is softer with you than Vic, and it lifts your heart that he has heard you. "Something bad happened in Minneapolis," you say. "Gus... wanted my help. But he—" Your voice is drowned out by a swell of synthesized horns and a wave of laughter from the crowd beyond the curtain—laughter swiftly followed by shocked gasps. Zorba's head swivels in that direction and he strides to the gap in the curtain and peeks out. You are forgotten. "Gus is having trouble," you insist, "I haven't seen him today but since Minneapolis he...." You trail off. Zorba isn't listening. "What is he *doing*," Zorba blurts, and the shock in his voice brings you up short. You shuffle to Zorba's side, your movements as graceless as your speech, and have a look for yourself.

Vinegar Vic has dropped his juggling pins. His painted eyebrows are raised so high they scrunch gently against his bald cap. His black lips are stretched into a long O of surprise that—this time—doesn't appear to be exaggerated for comic effect. You remember his pupils, blown black and dancing like flies on shit, and your first thought is that he's got the fear again. In Winnipeg, how Vic had screamed! What had he seen that night, in his bunk? Hands, that's right. Skeletal hands, creeping like lively spiders out of the big steamer trunk full of obscure pornographic magazines and weird sex toys he brings with him everywhere on the road. You'd had to feed him Oxy and vodka out of his kit bag until he had passed out in a sagging wooden chair. He'd still been painted white from his hairline to his nipples when he'd finally hunched over in drooling insensibility.

That was Winnipeg. Your first thought, then, as you peer past Zorba, is *Vic's having another bad trip, only this time in the spotlights.* But then you see Gus. As the auguste—or "red clown"—to Vic's white-faced, white-suited Pierrot, Gus' appearance in the ring should have occasioned merriment. The gag was for Gus to enter by tumbling head-over-heels into Vic, tipping him over. But that is not what has transpired.

Gus stands just inside the ring. He has emerged from the other side of the artists' entrance completely naked. From his broad, veiny feet, to the uncircumcised cock that dangles between his skinny thighs like a particularly unappetizing saucisson, to his long, sorrowful face, Gus is an unearthly shock-white—save for his mouth, which is surrounded by a large, sloppily-executed crimson smear.

One of Gus' hands is wrapped around the matte-black handle of his long straight razor. You've lingered near Gus' berth on many cross-country train rides as he stropped its edge before shaving—*whoosh-whip, whoosh-whip.*

The sound and the sway of the train were soothing, as was Gus' mellow, good-natured company. Now, the razor shines in the spotlights, its edge glittering like starlight on stagnant water. Gus' face wears an expression unlike any you've ever seen; ecstasy, lunacy, a rictus of unspeakable delight. His red-smeared lips are stretched in a grin so wide and rigid that you can see drool running freely from its edges; his eyes are wide, the conjunctiva a violent mottled red where his capillaries have burst.

Vic finds his voice. "What in the fuck do you think you're—" *Zip!* Gus brings the razor down in a sharp movement that is theatrical in its exaggerated negation, a referee signaling "no good!" Gus worked his way up to auguste on the strength of his mime work and tumbling, and whatever else has gone wrong with him, you think, he hasn't lost his gift for physical comedy.

The first slash catches Vinegar Vic across the broad front of his white silk suit. The suit is capacious, and Vic seems to subsist on little more than uppers and hard liquor, with periodic infusions of fried eggs. Fetching his laundry, you've seen him stripped down to stained boxer shorts; inside his white silk suit, he's all bone, lean muscle, and gristle. The razor misses the meat of him inside the suit completely on the first stroke—although you wouldn't know it to hear Vic bellow.

"You rat-dicked sonofabitch, this suit cost more than you—"

Gus flips the razor neatly in his hand. The second stroke is backhand, and opens Vic's face in a neat line from the corner of his chin, up through his lips and nose, and through one eye. For a single second that hangs in the air like a trapeze artist skating the limits of gravity, there is no blood. Then, as Vic brings his hands up to his howling face, there *is* blood. A great deal of blood. Against the white of Vic's greasepaint, it is so bright that Vic may as well be dropping handfuls of garnets onto the boards under the merciless spotlights.

Gus swivels on one bare heel and executes a nimble pirouette, cock and balls flapping against his thighs. The crowd howls. You can hear outrage in the rising tide of shouts, but there are gales of shocked laughter, too. You can't blame them—Gus is funny, and more than a little slapstick chaos has broken out in the stands. The synthesized score plays on and on, all ticklish cartoon xylophones and blatting ersatz trumpets—an automaton orchestra of the damned endlessly chasing its tail. Bill the sound man has abandoned his post. You can see him down in the stands, gangly arms waving about as he tries in vain to establish order.

At first, you don't recognize Gus' voice. "*Alleeeeeyyyy....OOP!*" he thunders, and kicks Vic in the balls. When Gus shouts, the sound is distorted: coarse, and so deep that it resonates in the middle of your stomach the way the sound system sometimes does. It doesn't sound like Gus. Not your gentle Gus, who grinned and murmured in your ear when you'd get flirty with him, and smelled like shave butter. That Gus can't be this manic, shock-white ghoul, naked and cavorting, bloody smear of a grin full of blunt little teeth.

But you know the lean contours of Gus' nude body too well to think it's anyone else. Even if the eyes are boiling whorls of blood in the milky cauldron of his face. Even if he seems to have too many teeth—so blunt, so small and crunched together—in too-wide of a rictus.

The kick from Gus has dropped Vic to the ground. Above him, Gus slashes and slashes. Vic's white suit comes away in long, bloody strips that sail back over Gus' head like the ribbons that the Russian dancers twirl—only these are sodden crimson instead of shimmering gold foil. The majority of the crowd has opted to flee. A few beefy rubes attempt to intervene instead and rush the floor. Gus moves with the grace of a ballerina. He dances from the pad of one bare foot to the ball of another, dragging the razor's glittering arc in his wake. "My fucking *eyes?!*" shrieks one rube, as another grips a spurting femoral artery and sinks to the boards, his blood abandoning him in buckets. The spotlights continue to circle the ring in a lazy figure-eight. Something in the sound booth has finally given in; the manic carnival music is replaced by shrill feedback from a live microphone abandoned somewhere.

Gus dances on and on, and you wonder *why is he so white?* Your speech is slow, your movements uncoordinated, and that has kept you sweeping floors and doing laundry in Circus Madrigal, but your *thoughts* have never been slow. No.

Were he performing as the auguste—the red clown—Gus should have been painted in flesh tones, with a bright—but neatly delineated—red-on-white mouth. The handle of Gus' razor is matte black and bloody in his grasp, unlike Vinegar Vic's cigarette butts, which had been smeared white by *his* paint. Gus hasn't left any footprints on the ring's wooden surface, nor any fingerprints on his razor's handle.

Gus isn't wearing greasepaint.

As you realize this, he turns his glittering eyes in your direction. You see nothing human in them. Vic raises his ruined face to the spotlights as though appealing to them for mercy. He convulses and spits a gout of blood. "Oh my God," Zorba says, his voice mild with shock, and your paralysis finally breaks. You turn and run for the exit, slow on your bad leg even in your panic.

You try to follow the inside curve of the canvas. Circus Madrigal styles itself as a living museum; practitioners of the old school, where even the tent itself is vintage, old cotton canvas instead of modern vinyl. The exits are packed with fleeing people—you watch as a boy, perhaps ten years old, stumbles and then falls beneath a throng of rushing, crushing feet.

A shrill scream rips the air behind you, and you spare a glance over your shoulder. Zorba is bent double cradling his hand, and blood is everywhere.

Gus meets your eyes and does a comic, theatrical spit take, spewing Zorba's fingers from between his ruby lips.

Suddenly you are aloft—lifted bodily and shoved along by the panicked flood of people. An elbow whacks your face, and you taste blood. You shift, struggle. You swing an awkward arm and feel your fist connect with someone's mouth, and then you are free, ejected from the flood of people and away from the exits, deeper under the big top. You limp and weep, stung by the crush of the crowd and terrified by Gus' eyes. Their vacancy and the depth of hungry mirth you'd seen there. A cackling ventriloquist dummy, both mindless and terribly *alive*.

Light flickers and you raise your bruised face. Of course your treacherous legs—operating by instinct, by habit—have brought you here, to the place where you and Gus rendezvous. His dressing room.

Gus has redecorated. There are tall candles—dozens of them, enough to fill the air with golden light. Also a new addition: black letters on the canvas walls, executed in manic finger-painted smears. IA VELES! And HAIL THE LAUGHER IN THE DARK, and JOLLY FELLOW OF THE ABBATOIR.

In the center of the candles, waiting atop Vic's old steamer trunk, a puff of blood-soaked wool. The lamb's head.

Everything before Minneapolis had been piling up, jammed and tangled in Gus' head. Vinegar Vic, his hard knuckles and whiplash voice—so vicious, so... *nasty*, the way he liked everything. And then in Minneapolis there'd been Vic's hard hands on Gus, the auguste, the second banana, once too often. That had torn it. Gustav Myasnyk, the only one of seven sons not to follow their father into the profession of butchery, had known whom to call upon and how. But he'd been afraid, at the end, had turned his head to the side and wept as you'd cut the lamb's throat so he could offer blood to Veles. You'd thought *well, he's mad, maybe, and the product of a superstitious upbringing.* You'd gone along with it anyway, willing to stifle your distaste. You were in love, and no stranger to slaughter from your childhood on the farm.

Here in what you still think of as your-and-Gus' hideaway, the lamb's head stares up at you from a shallow dish atop the steamer trunk. Its eyes are rolled back and its little pink tongue protrudes delicately from its black lips. You think of Vinegar Vic, cut to ribbons under the spotlights as a screaming crowd watched in horror. You feel sorry for the lamb, and for what Gus has become. But not for Vic.

There's a ringing in your ears, and a sharp *pull* as though an invisible fish hook in your mind were being tugged on from inside the trunk. The lamb looks up at you with mild-mannered surprise as you set the head and its dish aside. There's something in Gus' big steamer trunk—something he's left for you. You feel a terrible certainty about this. It feels like fate, and fate feels dead and cold and tastes like bitter ashes on your tongue. You carefully open the trunk.

It is empty—save for two one-gallon milk jugs, filled about three-quarters of the way each with congealing blood. Set into the bottom of the trunk's lid is a mirror, and in it, you see the thing wearing Gus enter the dressing room behind you. Now that Gus has drawn close—*so* close—you can see the cuts, the open wounds like toothless, thin-lipped mouths, open at wrist and wrist and neck. Gus has been bled dry, his blood left here as treasure, or perhaps tribute.

The voice behind you is as deep and as loud as a mountain's. "I'm thinking," it says, "we should workshop this next bit. Really take our time with it, you know?" You wonder how long Gus has been dead, his form worn by the thing he called "the holy goatherd." He wanted revenge, and now it has put him on like a costume—the ultimate clown suit, as it were. Its form stretches the confines of its host body. You can hear the creak and crack of Gus' jawbone fracturing as his mouth opens wider and wider. The crimson of his hemorrhaging eyes is bright. His eyes hold the last two spoonfuls of Gus' blood left in a bloodless, chalk-white corpse. His red-smeared lips are bright with the blood of others, though, and stretched so wide they split.

You kick the candles in a last act of negation. Fire and hot wax splash against canvas, and the walls go up with a flapping roar, a hot wind caught inside the tent that whips the air into a vortex of golden flames. The sound is tremendous, and drowns out the rising sound of distant screams. As Gus— or, rather, whatever cackling *thing* inhabits his carcass—sinks his teeth into your throat, you have time to think that it could be worse. At least the mouth tearing into you as the fire claims you both was dear to you, once.

It's not so lonely, this way.

————

Charles R. Bernard is a writer who lives in Salt Lake City. His work has appeared in several anthologies, including *Thuggish Itch* and *The Weird and Whatnot.*

Bag of Tricks

Joshua R. Smith

Leaking out from its split seams was an odor that smelled like a mix of stagnant bathwater and warm ketchup. "Come on, fifty bucks?" Peter Stance gave a disgusted snarl while looking over the frayed burlap sack that was barely held together by string and scraps. He was starting to wonder if this magic shop was worth the four-hour drive. "It's falling apart, man, an ant's fart could obliterate this thing."

"'An ant's fart?'" The owner of The Laughing White Rabbit Shop scoffed and pressed his loose-skinned index finger against the bag, "I assure you, sir, those fifty bucks will give you millions in magic." The old man's voice was rusted, caked from the decades of dust that he's been breathing in since opening the place.

"Uh huh," Peter rolled his eyes. "Millions of what, millions of scabies? Millions of parents asking me why their kids have pink eye after I opened this thing up and told them to '*go ahead and look inside*'?"

Laughing at Peter's aggressive judgement, the shopkeep took the same brittle finger he used to poke the bag and pointed to the wall behind the young entertainer. Pete turned and then felt his eyes dance to the song of unexpected amazement.

Bag of Tricks

Scattered from end to end, top to bottom were dozens of framed photos, each proudly holding sun faded images of the owner with iconic magicians, prop comics and those from Peter's profession, clowns. These were the greats. The people displayed on this wall were the ones that would make any joe-schmo who accidentally stumbled into this store look up and say, '*Oh shit, I know that guy!*' That was something beyond rare. That was something Peter had to have.

The shop owner looked to the wall over Peter's shoulder, he was living over the moments each photo was taken in under a nanosecond. "All these wonderful and successful people who have come to my shop and purchased this *bag of tricks* still use it in their acts to this day." He pursed away a smile as he remembered. "At least, if they're still with us anyway."

The gallery of legends was hard to deny. Some of them even held up their own variation of the bag proudly in their photos, like fisherman with a prize catch. Peter shook the sack with both hands and looked it over, feeling its weight and ignoring its smell he turned to the framed smiles one more time. "So this is like a bundle thing, fifty bucks and it just comes with random tricks and props?"

"No, no, no, no, no sir." The shopkeeper licked his cracked lips over and over, so much so that it made Peter's entire body cringe. "You see, it works off of the universe. Karma. Power. Fate." A loud pop came from his back as he leaned over the counter, taking the bag from the young man's hands.

A low echo of random noises came from the opening as the shopkeeper untied the drawstrings. Once fully opened he cocked his arm back, ready to dig in, but stopped just above it, he looked to Peter with his glossy brown eyes, "You have a handsome nose, sir." The crust to his vocal cords must have been wiped clean, because he sounded twenty years younger.

Joshua R. Smith

Peter said nothing. He scrunched his *handsome nose* and felt even more uncomfortable with the old man.

Another muffled wave of clatter came from the bag after the shopkeeper gave it a jostle and with a busted smile of gold and green teeth, he licked his dried lips several times over again and put his arm inside the bag. He winced after his hand hit the bottom. A tide of different emotions washed over his entire face as he rummaged through. First a look of pain, then disgust, sorrow, arousal, back to disgust and then finishing with another one of his grotesque colorful smiles.

"Oh." The old man stopped, his eyes screamed that he found something good from the top of their corneas. "Lookie lookie." A deep old giggle followed. "I think I got myself a big ol' cookie!" Pulling his arm from the bag, the man showed he was not joking. In his skeletal hands was the top curve of a giant cookie, which by Peters guess had to be at least four feet in diameter, "Looks to be an oatmeal raisin!" The old shopkeeper said while tipping out the large sweet from the bag, the cookie rolled across the room and wobbled to the floor.

"Holy shit!" Peter's eyes danced their second dance and he smiled. He couldn't believe it, but at the same time there it was. "How? I don't understand. Is there a trick hole, or did you fold it in there?"

"No, I think the stars just knew I wanted a sweet." The shopkeeper rubbed the white patchy stubble on his face, as he too looked in awe.

Peter snapped off a chunk and gave it a bite, "Holy shit. That's an actually a cookie." He said with a cold astonishment. Not waiting another minute, he dug for his wallet and pulled out his credit card. "Ok, man, fifty sounds cool."

The shopkeeper took the large piece of cookie from Peter and bit into the same spot. "Very cool," he said with crumbs spraying out of his mouth

191

and onto the counter. A few pieces stuck to the jagged dead flakes of his chapped lips and he licked them again. "*Very cool.*"

––––––––––

Eleven-year-old Leo Brinker was the first lucky kid to get to experience the newest addition to Pete's act. Peter knew it in his soul, this was the last shit birthday party he'd have to do. He knew soon enough he was going to have his own stage show, tour the country, possibly even get a regular gig in Vegas, or Atlantic City in a couple of years and not have to stand in some tiny living room for another two hour bullshit set. He was going to be out of the suburbs and on the road, only to come back to this part of the country once a year for a random gig and then obviously stop to get his photo taken for The Laughing White Rabbits wall of legends.

He pulled up to the house. Predictable, little Leo Brinkers home was just like all the others. It hosted a perfect lawn with several neighborhood bikes tossed on top of it. A freshly washed SUV and a garage that was left proudly open, flaunting all of dad's tools, rifles, weights, and a disassembled vintage motorcycle of some kind. It was the kind of bike Peter had dreamed of having since he was sixteen, but fuck it, those dreams would be replaced by better ones soon enough.

"Prick," Peter snarled while parking his primer grey hatchback around the corner of the house, its engine rattling an extra few seconds after he turned it off. He sighed, pulled down the vanity mirror and looked over his makeup. His white pancaked face was even, red nose centered and the blue hair that curled from the sides felt extra funky. He said it again, the sixteenth time this drive, "This is it." The one that will get him on the Channel Six News, then viral, and on the road.

Stepping out of the car, Pete bit at the bottom of his large white gloves, pulling them tightly onto his fingers before grabbing the bag, his trunk of props and stomping his big green shoes to the door. On his way, he snorted and hocked a thick loogie and spat it onto the motorcycle parts laying in the garage. "Vroom vroom, bitch."

The front door was a pleasant dark blue that had a perfectly contrasted brass door knocker centering it. Peter used the knocker as a final mirror, checking his teeth for any lipstick. All clear. Before knocking he reached in the bag for one final test, even though all week he's been amazed by the contents inside, no matter how painful some of them were. He dug around while still looking at his reflection in the knocker and continued until a hard pinch met his wrist. "Fuck!"

Yanking his hand out from the bag, he found a small crawdad clamped tightly to him. Right before Peter continued to scream his swears the front door opened and standing just a few inches over him was, by his guess, Leo's father.

"Hey there, I got some butter inside if you want to boil that little guy up." The man chuckled and put his hand out to Pete. "Lance Brinker, nice to meet-"

"Pesky Pete!" Peter goofily interrupted and before he put his hand out he yanked the crawdad from his arm and dropped it back in the bag.

"Great stuff," Lance laughed with real enjoyment. "So the kids are out back in the pool. Did you want to set up back there or somewhere specific?"

"Oh no, sir," Pesky Pete continued with his signature yokel clown voice, "Anywhere is a just fine, yup yup!"

Lance smiled again and revealed that his inner child was crashing his son's party. "Yup yup!" He echoed and showed Pesky Pete in. "Do you need a hand with your stuff?"

"Ah nope nope, sir, you can get a back to your par-tay-ing and I'll just set up shop right in the living room."

"Awesome," Lance gave Pete a firm pat on the shoulder, "I'll wrangle up the kids in fifteen?"

"Perfecto muchacho!"

The young father gave Pesky Pete a strong thumbs-up and walked to the back screen door, stopping to talk to a few guests while also wrangling up the kids.

"Fucking tool," Pete whispered and began to set up his props and pump air into a few magic balloons. He decided to stick with the same opener he'd been using for the last few years and make his newest purchase the grand finale.

Within fifteen minutes, kids and parents were filling up the room. It was easily the biggest turnout Pete had had with any of his shows in the last two or even three years. The butterflies were fluttering and he welcomed them with a bright red smile.

"Howdy doo doo, kids!"

The room erupted with small innocent laughter, these kids knew good humor when they heard it and a shit joke will always be good humor.

The act went off without a hitch, the highs and lows met their marks and it was finally time for wrap up, the grand finale. The bag of tricks.

"Ok, boys and hurls, are you ready to see Pesky Pete's newest purchase?"

"Yeah!" they screamed in unison. This was the perfect crowd for the suburban bullshit. They sat still, they laughed and none of them felt the need to cry, fuck with the props, or worse fall asleep.

"That's what I'm talking about!" Like a drunken ballerina, Pesky Pete spun a full sloppy pirouette, knocking over his trunk of props and falling to his ass. Cue the laughs.

Pesky Pete then opened his trunk, playfully tossing props over his shoulder at the kids, hitting them with rubber chickens, fake puke and candy, before finally pulling out the burlap bag. "I picked this up from a hairy man in Kazakhstan," Both the kids and the parents laughed. "Or was it from a chicken salesman in Turkey?" The second line wasn't as good as the first, but there were still some giggles.

Pesky Pete held the bag behind his back, waiting to reveal. "I present to you—"

He stopped and squinted at the kids, "Drum roll please," he whispered. The kids patted on the carpet, their faces beaming now as they felt like they were part of the show. Pesky Pete danced to their beat for a moment and then abruptly stopped. They stopped with him.

He arched his trademark clown smile and then held the bag up in the air with one hand to the seventy-five watt heavens, shouting with a deep and epic voice, "Pesky Pete's bag of tricks!"

The kids looked unimpressed, some even grossed out by its stains and how old it was. "Isn't it just beautiful?"

"No," One of the boys sitting in front answered back right away. His dry response made some of the parents burst out an uncontrolled laugh, Pete's stomach sank, but their skepticism would soon change.

The clown's smile dropped and he stepped slowly to the kids, closing one of his eyes as he looked them over interrogatively, "Who said that?" His clown voice had disappeared when asking the question, he noticed the flub and so did some of the parents as they now watched him closely, wondering if he actually took offense to the answer.

"He did! He did!" Picking herself up from the carpeted floor, a little blonde girl with bright pink overalls poked the top of a boys head with her index finger over and over.

Bag of Tricks

The kid had a large scab on his chin and an adorable smudge of chocolate under his left eye. He swatted the girl away. "Stop, Amy!" But his focus on her quickly vanished as Pesky Pete was now nose to red nose with him.

"You don't like my new bag, buster?" Pesky Pete asked in a playful ready-to-fight tone.

"It's ugly!" the little boy said right back at him.

Pesky Pete clutched his invisible pearls and gasped, "How dare you! This bag holds all the magic in the universe between its seams."

"No it doesn't!" the boy spat back.

"Yeah huh!"

"Nuh-uh!"

"Yeah huh!"

"Nuh-uh!"

They went back and forth and the tension thinned, the room filled back up with laughs again.

"Ok." Pesky Pete opened the bag and shook it up, random sounds of pots and pans, glass breaking, and cows mooing came out of the opening. "Why don't you reach inside then."

The kid now looked nervous; he didn't want to show it, so he swallowed the fear, nodded and stood up.

"Alright, Dax!" Lance shouted out and clapped, the rest of the parents followed suit as the boy got to his feet.

"So, your name is Dax?"

"Yeah,"

"Ok, Dax, what I want you to do is put your arm in the bag and grab the first thing ya feel, do you think you could do that?"

"Sure" Dax shrugged, ready to get this over with.

"'Sure', ok cool," Pesky Pete was acting like he was too cool for this whole thing too. "Yeah, whatever," Only the parents laughed at this. It was always nice to see a little smartass get mocked every once in a while.

Dax rolled his sleeve up to his elbow and got to his tiptoes, but before his hand went in Pesky Pete grabbed his wrist. "But, before you go digging around in there, you gotta say the magic words."

"What are the magic words?" Dax shrugged again, his voice back to the adorable curious tone of a young boy.

"You gotta say, '*Pesky Pete is the cooooooolest clown in town*,'" A few kids and parents giggled. Dax scrunched his nose and looked at Pete like he was an idiot, "You gotta make sure you say those words or the bag won't work." Pesky Pete then pretended to bite the nails of his gloves, showing his concern on how important it was to say these words.

"Pesky Pete is the coolest clown in town." Dax said flatly.

"Oh, no, no, no, no, no, Dax. Say it with a little heart," Pesky Pete clenched his fist and shook it in the air, "Say it like the man I know you are!"

"Pesky Pete is the coolest clown in town."

"Louder, Dax!"

"Pesky Pete is the coolest clown in town." Parents began to clap and hoot, helping Dax to liven up.

"I can't hear you!" Pete said while leaning in and cupping around an ear.

Dax inhaled deeply and shouted out as loud as he could, "PESKY PETE IS COOLEST CLOWN IN TOWN!"

"There it is!" The clown shouted back and the room erupted, the kids looked to the adults and clapped as hard as they could.

"Ok." Pesky Pete lowered the bag to Dax's reach, "Pick me a winner, kiddo."

Bag of Tricks

The boy was feeling it now, he gave a hard nod before diving his arm shoulder deep into the bag. The random sounds came again as he scoured through. Then, the kids' eyes widened when his tiny hands finally caught something.

"What do you got for me, Dax my boy?"

The boys face reddened and scrunched in pain before letting out a high-pitched scream. The little ones circling around them looked confused. Parents put down their paper plates of birthday cake and went to see what was wrong, or to pull their own children away to safety.

Pete didn't know what was happening, he along with two of the fathers by him, pulled Dax's arm from the burlap bag. The boy sobbed and begged, "Stop it! Owww! Stop, it hurts! It hurts! Mom! Mom, it's cold!" The bag fell to the ground and Dax's arm was revealed for everyone at Leo Brinker's eleventh birthday party to see.

A small blue arm stretched out, ice blue and transparent from the shoulder down. The boy wept and sobbed, his mother running towards him, she wanted to hold his arm, but didn't know if it would shatter from her touch.

"Oh my god, sweetie, hold still ok? Just hold still for mommy," Her voice trembled and did little to comfort her son. She looked to anyone for help, but all the other parents could do was grab their own kids, hold them tightly and watch her be as lost as they would be if it happened to them. Lance on the other hand went charging towards the clown, grabbing him by the bright orange suspenders and slamming him to the wall.

"What the fuck is this?" He pressed himself against Peter.

"I-I-I don't know, this has never happened before. I swear to God," Pete stammered. He didn't know it, but he was still talking in his clown voice.

"Stop talking like that!" one of the mothers screamed.

191

Pete put both his hands up. "I'm sorry. I'm sorry." He looked to the bag on the floor, its opening pouring out a frosted fog and then he looked to little Dax, the boy with the icicle for an arm. Some parents tried to comfort him and his mother, others called for nine-one-one, then there was one question that stopped them all from what they were doing.

"What's that say on his arm?" Asked the father of the little blonde girl who was poking Dax on the head just two minutes ago.

"Oh my god, there's words chiseled into his arm." Said another parent.

"What's it say?" Lance asked, his fists still clenched onto Pete and his weight pressing the clown even harder to the wall.

One of the fathers who was helping comfort Dax looked to Lance and then to the clown with horror and anger, "It says, '*Pesky Pete is the coolest clown in town.*'"

Pete felt the moisture in his mouth dry up. His dreams of touring, TV appearances and Las Vegas hotel shows melted away in the suburban living room with little Dax's fingers and as he looked back to the bag he was certain he heard the sandpaper sound of crusted old lips being licked.

Joshua R. Smith is an aspiring writer from central Ohio. Since childhood his love for horror, science fiction and fantasy have flooded his thoughts and now that love spills out from his fingertips and onto the pages. For more information you can follow him on Instagram and Twitter @WriteJoshWrite.

Alas, Poor Yorick

G.K. Lomax

What makes a clown laugh?

You might think that a foolish question. A clown, you might declare, is a man like any other; he laughs at that which makes other men laugh, surely?

Not so. This was the most important—and the most painful—lesson that my master taught me. A clown never laughs. It is his calling to make other men laugh, but he must never do so himself. A clown follows the most serious of all professions—and the most miserable.

My name is Osric, and at the age of eight or nine (I have never known my exact age) I was prenticed to Yorick, clown to King Hamlet at Elsinore. How came I so? I was a foundling, bereft of kin, and a burden on the city. At the May Fair, I and my companions in misfortune were made to stand on the Prentice Block to see if any master would be prepared to assume responsibility for us.

I stood there for most of the day, with nothing to eat or drink. My fellows were taken on one by one—by a carpenter, a tanner, a cordwainer and others—but not I. I didn't know what would happen if no-one wanted me, but I was sure it was nothing good. I foresaw a beating and precious little to eat.

About an hour before sunset, when most of the tradesmen where shutting up their stalls, a man came and studied me intently. He was a strange scarecrow of a man, with wild hair and protruding teeth. He struck me as being oddly proportioned, as though made up of ill-matching parts. His head was too big for his body, his legs too short, and one of his arms looked longer than the other. His manner of dress was odd, also. His coat seemed to be made up entirely of patches, each of a different colour, and his boots were over-large. He carried a staff, with a cluster of small bells tied to its top.

He stared at me for a long time. His eyes were large, pale blue and watery. They seemed to me to be very sad. I couldn't guess what profession the man followed, but it was clearly not one that gave him joy, nor one that had made him prosperous. I thought he might be a layer-in of the dead, and wondered if it was to be my fate to deal with corpses until I became one myself.

He stared at me for a long time. What did he see? A small, gangling and ugly child; feeble, half-starved—and plainly terrified. To stand on the Block was ordeal enough, but the man's silent stare multiplied my fears a hundred fold. My leg began to twitch, and the more I tried to control it the more it jerked and quivered. I felt as though I was about to burst into tears. I also felt as though my bladder would burst—I had, as I've said, been standing motionless all day.

"What's your name, boy?" the man asked suddenly.

I opened my mouth to answer, but could form no words.

"Your name?" the man repeated.

"Os... Osr-r-r-" I stammered.

"His name is Osric, kind sir," the Master of Foundlings put in, clearly wishing to be rid of me so that he could pack up and go home.

"Osric, eh?" the scarecrow said, looking at me rather than my master.

"Answer, boy" my master prompted impatiently.

"Y...ye..." It was all I could manage. I burst into tears. As if in sympathy, my bladder gave up the struggle and I voided myself.

There was a long pause. I stood there mute, warm piss pooling round my bare feet, feeling as miserable as I'd ever felt. I braced myself for the worst beating of my life.

Then the scarecrow said, "He'll do."

———————

Thus began my apprenticeship with my master, Yorick. It was hard. Not that my master was cruel—he only ever beat me once—but there was much to learn. First came tumbling, for a clown must be something of an acrobat. Indeed, he must be more than something. My master always insisted that it was necessary to learn how to do something surpassing well before it was possible to do it badly. After tumbling came juggling, then sleight of hand and other trickeries.

At these physical skills I proved tolerably adept, and made sufficient progress to satisfy my master. Other skills came less easily. Songs for example —memorising old ones and composing new ones extempore. There were whole days when my master forbad me to speak unless it was in perfect rhyme. As for jests and other flashes of merriment—my master applied his fundamental principle to this sphere as well, telling me it required very sharp wits to pass oneself off as a half-wit.

And the one beating? It came some two months into my training. I told my master a joke of my own devising. It was about a duck. He nodded, and said that it had merit.

Pleased with myself, I laughed. And my master beat me.

"You. Must. Never. Laugh," he told me between strokes of the switch. "It is the business of a clown to make others laugh, but he must never do so himself. Never. Never. Never." Thwack. Thwack. Thwack.

"Listen," my master said, throwing the switch into a corner and continuing in a milder tone. "Why do men laugh?"

"Because they find something funny?"

"And what do men find funny above all?"

"Jests?"

"No."

There was a long, painful pause. "I don't know, Master," I admitted eventually.

"Men laugh at the misery of others. If a man falls in the street and hurts himself, do not others laugh at him? If a man is walking unawares and steps in a pile of dung, are his companions not amused? When a felon is to be hanged, do not crowds gather to enjoy his terror and his agony? Man is cruel. All men are cruel.

"This is the lesson a clown must take to heart. When your tumbling seems to go wrong, don't spring to your feet with a smile. Make the company think that you fell through lack of skill, not deliberately; and though I've taught you how to fall without hurting yourself, you must always act as though you have. *Then* they will laugh. If some drunken carouser pours a flagon of Rhenish on your head, don't share the jest. Bewail your lot, and that will set the table on a roar."

My master came and sat close by me, and his tone became kindly. "Do you know why I chose you to be my prentice?"

"No, Master."

"I chose you because you have known misery. Indeed, you have known nothing but. You don't know who your parents were, do you?"

"No, Master."

"No more do I know the names of mine. My youth was much like yours. You were raised as a foundling, at the city's expense—and the city is far from open-handed in such matters. You were often beaten, often cold, always hungry and dressed in rags. Is this not so?"

"Yes, Master."

"And at the May Fair you stood all the day on the Prentice Block, watching in despair as your fellows were chosen one by one—until you alone remained. True?"

"Yes, Master."

"Then when I stood before you you felt terror and wet yourself. Also true?"

Colour rose to my face—I had been trying to forget that shame. I could only nod.

"Yes, you have known misery," my master said, "and that is why you will make a great clown."

———

It was many months before my master considered me skilled enough to perform in public, but he did arrange for me to watch him at work. He had a word with the steward, and since the latter could always use another serving-boy I was admitted to the feasts, where it was my job to scamper to and fro with jugs of ale and wine and mead, ensuring that no goblet was ever empty. Not the King's goblet, of course—he had his own cup-bearer—but I was kept busy enough. My main duty, however, was to watch my master, observing his performance at close hand. Sometimes he would "accidentally" stumble into me and send me sprawling on the floor. This always got a laugh, especially if I rose soaked in ale.

Once I forgot my training and fell badly, bloodying my nose—which provoked a bigger laugh. On another occasion I managed (deliberately) to smash a pitcher as I fell. I sat in a puddle of wine looking downcast. With all eyes on me, I reached behind my back for a shard and drew it forth with a jerk and a wail, as though it had been impaled in my rear. This provoked the loudest laugh yet. Then, struck with inspiration, I held up the broken handle of the pitcher and said, "Have a care, Master Yorick, Master Steward will have the cost of this pitcher out of my hide," and burst into tears.

That was the first time I "Set the table on a roar" (a favourite phrase of my master). They clapped and banged the table, and a couple even threw coppers at me.

Yes, men will laugh at the misery of others.

My master had not neglected to introduce me to those he entertained. Well, not introduce as such. He led me up to a small space in the eaves of the Great Hall, where we could lay on our stomachs and peer at the great folk below without being seen.

"That is King Hamlet," my master told me, "and that is Queen Gertrude. The boy close by them is their son, Young Hamlet."

I studied the young prince. He was perhaps two years older than I, and richly dressed. Nevertheless, I thought there was something odd about him. After a while, it came to me that he seemed too serious. Like most paupers, I'd dreamt about what it would be like to be rich—never to be cold or hungry, never to have to wear clothes that were threadbare or stained, always to have servants anxious to do one's bidding. I'd imagined that in such a state I'd always be laughing and happy—yet here was Young Hamlet looking sad and subdued. It was unaccountable. He could not, I thought, have known misery, so why was it written on his face?

"The King," my master continued, "is mostly easy to please, especially after his third flagon. If all else fails, a face full of pie will make him laugh. Waste not your subtleties on him, though the Queen will appreciate them. She and the King's brother, Lord Claudius. That's him there. Mark him well. He's sharper than the King, and more cruel. Be sure that you make no jest at his expense, for he'll make you pay dearly for it."

"But—" I began.

"There are no buts," my master said, forestalling me. "Yes, at the start of each evening I beg formal forgiveness from the King, and am granted licence, as you will be in due time; but this will count for nothing with Claudius if you overstep the bounds in his eyes. Never forget that. Now, as for the rest of the company..."

Quickly, my master pointed out the other nobles assembled—Cornelius, Voltimand, Horatio, Rosencrantz, Guildenstern—with a brief summary of their likes and dislikes when it came to entertainment. "Now I must go and earn my keep," he said. "You remain here and watch."

"Wait, Master," I protested, "There's one lord you've not named. Him of the black jerkin and forked beard."

"That," my master said, slowly, "is Polonius. He's Claudius' creature. If you ever make him laugh at anything, may I be there to witness it."

Miserable as my life may have been up until that point, I still possessed a natural childish curiosity. Why, I thought, did a man—a rich man, a noble man, seemingly in favour with the king—never laugh? I resolved to find out.

For a week or so, I dogged Polonius' footsteps whenever I could. This was surprisingly often. Though my master trained me hard, he was also prone to fits of melancholy when he would be alone, leaving me with naught to occupy myself for a few hours. I had already begun to use this free time to explore great Elsinore, poking my nose into as many places as possible. No-one ever stopped me to enquire about my business—as the meanest of all the servants I was beneath the notice of my betters, who in any case would simply assume that I was running some errand if I chanced to cross their path.

Polonius was accounted learned and wise, the first among the King's counsellors and the one who most often had the King's ear. He lived a sparse life. He dressed always in sober black, and seemed to have no taste for jewellery or other tokens of wealth and status. He drank within moderation and was never drunk. He kept but one personal servant—Reynaldo, a taciturn foreigner whose sharp gaze seemed to miss nothing—and retired each night to a chamber that others of his rank would've considered insultingly small. I never dared to set foot in it, but did once manage to steal a glance inside. Polonius possessed many books, and to judge by the piles of parchment on his table, did much writing.

He was a widower, though he had two children—a son and a daughter—who lived apart from him in the care of tutors and a nurse. The son, Laertes, was the nearest thing Young Hamlet had to a playmate. The daughter, Ophelia, was rarely seen.

One thing that was obvious about Polonius was that he was not loved. Rather, he seemed to be feared. I'm not speaking of servants—we whose livelihoods hang by a thread should we ever give offense. I mean that even those with noble blood were cold towards him, and wary in his presence, as if they suspected that he was a man of stratagems who was plotting their fall. Mayhap they were right.

There was nothing in all of this, however, to explain the mystery of why Polonius never laughed. This left me unsatisfied. Then, one cold and rainy afternoon when all who could were sheltering indoors, I chanced to see him crossing the courtyard in haste. He opened a door that led to the outer ward, and passed through. I can't say what it was, but it seemed to me that there was something strange in his manner. Thinking that he might lead me to the answers I sought, I followed him.

Elsinore stands on a promontory overlooking the straits that separate Denmark from the land of the Geats. The outer ward slopes downwards to the sea wall, in the lee of which are a number of store-rooms and workshops. The northernmost of these nestles in an angle of the wall caused by it following the line of the land. As such, it is mostly hidden from view. This room Polonius approached. Had he glanced over his shoulder he would've seen me, but the rain was heavy and made him hurry. He produced a large key and entered. I hesitated long but eventually, torn between fear and fascination, I crept nearer, hauled myself up to the one small window and peered over the sill. The window was shuttered and barred, but there was a small crack through which I could see part of the room.

Polonius had lit a lantern, though it cast little light. Slowly, my eyes penetrated the gloom and I made out a table on which was a clutter of glass vessels, filled with liquids of various hues. The sort of collection, I thought, that an alchemist would possess. This made sense to me—alchemy can produce noxious smells that might well have caused a practitioner to be banished to a distant part of the castle.

In front of the tables stood a small brazier, glowing hot. Polonius himself was not in my line of sight, but I could hear him muttering to himself. This went on for some time but at length he placed one of the vessels on the brazier. A dark liquid was within.

Polonius' muttering continued, getting gradually louder. It seemed to me that there was a distinct rhythm to it. Then it came to me—not a mutter but a chant. Was Polonius was a sorcerer? Appalled, I continued to stare, and saw a vapour start to rise from the vessel on the brazier. A vapour that coiled and swirled and seemed to assume fantastical shapes...

Fighting the urge to scream, I dropped from the window and fled.

———————

I never breathed a word of what I'd seen, not even to my master. I tried hard to convince myself that the form I'd seen had been imagination, and that Polonius was an alchemist—nothing more. As the weeks and months passed, I almost came to believe it.

Meanwhile, I applied myself to learning my trade and was finally permitted to Don the Motley. That is to say, I dressed myself in a clown's attire and began to participate more fully in the revels. And not before time, either, for my master was beginning to get old. Even over the half year since he'd taken me on, I'd noticed that there was less spring in his capering, and he often complained of stiffness the morning after a feast. His wits were still sharp, though, and he set the table on a roar more times than I could count.

I meanwhile was his foil, his stooge, a fool's fool. I was the butt of jokes, and the one who took the most seemingly painful falls. Yet I was more than that. It took me some time to realise it, but my master was as sad and as lonely as any man has ever been. To him, therefore, I was more than a prentice, more than someone to whom he could pass on his skills. I was the nearest he would ever come to having a son.

There was another reason he employed me as well. As one well-versed in misery, he could detect it in others. He detected it—as I had—in Young Hamlet, and sought to lighten the gloom that hung heavy on those young shoulders. He thought that a young clown would be a good physic for a young prince; and in some measure he was right. Young Hamlet did smile and laugh betimes, even if not as often as we thought good for him.

One of our most successful plays in that regard was that of the mock hunt. I would be the prey, and Young Hamlet would be enlisted as the huntsman, mounted pig-a-back on my master, who would serve as his steed. Round and round the hall I'd lead the chase, hopping over stools and scampering under tables with Young Hamlet whooping and the rest cheering him on, until at last I was brought to bay. In time it became a favourite— even an expected—part of the entertainment, to be enacted night after night. My master once said to me that he expected to bear Young Hamlet on his back a thousand times before he was full grown.

———————

Years passed. Young Hamlet reached his fifteenth year and underwent the ceremony welcoming him to manhood, proudly stroking the small hairs new-sprouted on his chin. I supposed I was not far behind him, though there would be little ceremonial for me. By this time I was established as a clown in my own right, though my master and I usually performed together.

It was also at this time that war came. Fortinbras, proud and grasping King of Norway, had long coveted Danish lands, and often raided them. This led to retaliations and counter-retaliations, until nothing but a full-scale battle would satisfy honour on either side. I joined the crowd that cheered lustily as King Hamlet's fleet sailed past Elsinore and out into the open sea.

I cheered even louder when he returned a month later, having won a great victory. Ten Norwegian ships were sunk, it was said, and the rest put to flight. Better yet, the villain himself was drowned—though his son, Young Fortinbras, escaped.

You may wonder why I, a simple clown, concerned myself with such matters. It was because a clown must know the business of his masters, in order to amuse them the better. At the celebration feast—which lasted until dawn—my master and I appeared barefoot and haggard, clutching broken spears. Assuming his most bovine expression, my master announced "King Fortinbras am I, and this—" pointing at me "—my proud host of warriors..." upon which the company hurled both abuse and foodstuffs at us, to general mirth. Even Young Hamlet laughed—though Polonius did not.

The celebrations—and the drinking—lasted, as I say, until dawn. The sun rose to see King Hamlet slumped in his chair and snoring, and most of the rest of the company lying equally insensible in corners or under tables. This was the hour—when the feast was over, I mean—when we lesser folk were permitted to make what we would of whatever remained. A rib of beef here, a cup of ale there. Usually I was industrious in finding tasty scraps that had been overlooked, but the hour being so late (or so early) on this occasion, I did no more than take a mouthful or two before leaving the hall.

Weary as I was, I didn't make straight for my bed. The fires in the Great Hall had been roaring all night, producing a great deal of smoke. I felt the need for unsullied air to clear my head, so I made for the courtyard. When I got there, I saw Polonius and Lord Claudius holding an earnest conversation.

I say conversation, but that is not the right word. I was not near enough to hear what was being said, but it was clear that Polonius was displeased with Lord Claudius, and was haranguing him—poking him in the chest to emphasise each point he made. Despite his more exalted rank,

Lord Claudius bore all in meek silence, his eyes downcast.

I withdrew into the shadow behind a pillar so as not to be seen, for I did not think it would profit me to be noticed. I ought to have left entirely, but I could not take my eyes off the scene, which went on for some time. I was not near enough to hear what was said, other than one phrase which Polonius uttered in exasperation: "Yes, it must be both. You have waited too long for it to be otherwise. Both, and soon."

This made no sense to me, but I told master what I'd witnessed. "I thought you told me," I said, "that Polonius was Lord Claudius' creature, not the other way round."

My master took some time to answer. "Polonius is a spider who spins his own web," he said at last. "He is Lord Claudius' creature when it suits him to be. He aims to be more than that, however."

"What do you mean?" I asked.

My master sighed. "You are young," he told me, "but perhaps it is time that you learnt about politics."

"Politics?"

"Intrigue, whispers, foul designs masked behind fair visages. The means by which a man plots his own rise and the fall of his rivals. The whole business of the court, in fact."

"Is Polonius plotting the fall of Lord Claudius?" I asked.

"No, his rise."

"How so?"

"It is safer for you not to know."

"But Master—"

"Peace!"

There was a long painful silence. I feared at first that I'd earned my second beating, but it was not so. After a while my master calmed himself, and resumed in a more measured tone.

"Very well, Osric, attend. Lord Claudius may be the brother of King Hamlet, but there is little love between them. You must have observed this."

"A little. I thought it no great matter."

"That is because Lord Claudius hides his true feelings well. But not well enough. Know this: there are two reasons for his hatred—aye, hatred; it is not too strong a word. The first is natural enough, which is that the council chose Hamlet over Claudius to be king when their father, King Horwendil, died—before you were born, I dare say."

"But that was the natural choice, surely?" I asked. "King Hamlet is the elder brother."

"Aye—but the resentment of younger sons has caused much strife since the world was made, and will ever do so."

"I see. And the second reason?"

"Can you not guess?"

"No, Master."

"No? Perhaps you are still too young. It is the matter of the King's wife."

"Queen Gertrude?"

"She. You are surely aware that a king—or a king's son—takes a wife for reasons of policy, not love. Queen Gertrude is of the royal house of the Geats, whose king desired an alliance with King Horwendil. To seal the bargain, he offered his daughter as wife to Lord Hamlet, as he was then. King Horwendil accepted, as he was bound to do, and the nuptials were duly solemnised. But matters fell out ill. When Lord Claudius laid eyes on the Lady Gertrude, he lusted after her—and she after him, or so gossip has it. That, they say, is why Lord Claudius has never taken a wife, though he has often been urged to do so—for reasons of policy—by his brother.

"That the King and the Queen love each other not is no great novelty. Nor is the fact that the King takes his pleasures elsewhere. Most kings do. That Lord Claudius greatly desires something that the King possesses without valuing it, however—that is a weeping sore that will only be cured with the death of one party or the other."

"Does the King know this?"

"He would be a fool if he did not—and he's no fool."

"So why does he not take action?"

"Against his brother? He dare not. It would tear the Kingdom in half. Lord Claudius has not—so far as is known—committed any treasonable act. So long as he does not do so, King Hamlet cannot raise his hand against him for fear of provoking a deal of his Lords into crying 'Vengeance' and rising up against him. Rosencrantz and Guildenstern surely would, and maybe others."

"And Polonius?"

"Polonius is more subtle—and more ambitious. That he is valued by the King is not enough for him. He wants to govern, not to advise. He cannot be King—he is not of royal blood. But he can govern *through* a King. A King who is beholden to him, in thrall to him, who will do his bidding. And for that he needs to place Claudius on the throne, or so it's whispered."

"I see. Could not the King banish Lord Claudius? Such things have been done before."

"Aye, they have. But where would Claudius go? To Norway, without doubt. There he would pour his poison into the ear of Fortinbras, and enlist his aid in overthrowing and supplanting his brother. There is even a rumour —just a rumour, mark you; nothing proven—that the war just past was provoked by Lord Claudius. That he invited Fortinbras to commit himself, promising him a share of the spoils. Had Norway prevailed in battle, it is whispered, Lord Claudius would have raised the banner of rebellion from within, and King Hamlet would've been caught between two fires."

I thought about this for a while. I must confess that my chief thought was that Young Hamlet's melancholy might be caused by the fact that there was no affection between his father and his mother, and that he'd grown up knowing the sorrow of a loveless family. After a while, however, a more obvious question occurred to me.

"But what was the meaning of what Polonius said to Lord Claudius?"

"I do not know, and fear to guess. Now no more questions."

From that moment I was a spy almost as much as I was a clown, and observed the doings of the court with a different eye. On the surface, all was well. The Kingdom was secure, now that its chief foe had been vanquished; and prosperous with the tribute Young Fortinbras had been obliged to pay. But beneath the surface, I now realised, there were strange currents.

The most obvious change was that King Hamlet now surrounded himself more closely with his guards. He had always been thus attended, of course, but hitherto that had been a question of status and ceremony. Now it seemed to me that safety and security were the watchwords. At least three guards stood withing touching distance at all times. It seemed to me that an assassin would not find it easy to get close enough to the King.

An assassin with a dagger, that is. There were, as I was well aware, other ways of committing murder. Poison for one—but since the King's food and drink were always publicly tasted before he partook of them, he seemed safe from that quarter. Which left...

More and more, the memory of what I'd seen in Polonius' alchemical workshop returned to haunt me. Eventually, I decided that I would need to learn more. One night, therefore, I made my way to the row of store-rooms in the outer ward. I didn't waste time with Polonius' locked door or shuttered window, but entered the next room along. It didn't seem to be much used, containing little other than a clutter of broken barrels and empty sacks. I'd brought a candle with me and, after fumbling a while with my flint, I lit it and held it high. The wall separating me from Polonius' workshop was of solid stone. The floor was of beaten earth, and looked as though it would be the work of many hours, if not days, for me to dig a tunnel. The roof, however, was a different matter.

Nimble as an acrobat—or a clown—I scrambled up into the rafters. The roof was of thatch and, after feeling around for a few moments (I wasn't foolish enough to carry a lighted candle close to easily burnable thatch), I found what I sought. At the highest point, the dividing wall didn't quite rise to the level of the roof, leaving a small space. Though I was slender of figure, I saw that I would have to enlarge it a little, and set to work hauling handfuls of thatch out of the underside of the roof.

I was still engaged in doing so when the door to the workshop opened and Polonius entered, followed by Lord Claudius.

I froze, scarcely daring to breathe. I prayed neither man would look up, though even with the light of the lantern Lord Claudius carried, the eaves were deep in shadow. Polonius closed the door and locked it, then turned to Lord Claudius.

"You asked for proofs. Here you shall see them."

"Here? I see nothing but alchemists' toys, and alchemists are naught but tricksters."

Polonius didn't reply directly to that. Instead he gestured towards the brazier, from which flames instantly leapt up.

Lord Claudius gasped. "Sorcery?"

"Magic," replied Polonius. "Or trickery, if you prefer"

"You meddle with dark powers," Lord Claudius said. He sounded a lot less sure of himself. "That is dangerous indeed."

"More dangerous than treason? More dangerous than plotting to murder your brother, the King? More dangerous than bedding the King's anointed

Queen?"

"Enough. Show me these proofs. Tell me how you intend to proceed."

"By pouring poison into the King's ear."

"What?" Lord Claudius roared, sure of himself again. "I tried that with Fortinbras of Norway, and that turned out ill."

"You mistake me, Lord Claudius," Polonius said in an oily tone. I got the impression that he was enjoying himself more than somewhat. I wondered if I would actually hear him laugh. "You mistake the meaning of the phrase. When I say that I mean to pour poison into your brother's ear, I am not speaking figuratively. I am not referring to malicious hints and devious falsehoods, designed to make your quarry will act as you wish. I spoke more to the point. Poison in the King's ear. Poison that will trickle into his brain and cause a burning. A burning that will eat away at his reason, drive him mad, so that he will attempt to rend his own body all to pieces. A poison, furthermore, that will befoul the thin and wholesome blood that courses through his veins, which impure blood, when it passes through the natural gates of his heart, will stop it as it were a stone."

I almost gasped at this point. Who would've thought that there was a poetic touch to Polonius' villainy?

Lord Claudius didn't seem to appreciate it, though. "Very well; poison, with an outward appearance of madness and seizure. I won't ask which of these vessels contains so loathsome a brew. But there must be more to your schemes."

"There is. This wouldn't have been required, had you acted earlier, but since Young Hamlet has come of age..."

In a flash, I had it. When I'd heard Polonius say "It must be both," he had been referring to the murders of both the King and Young Hamlet. Had the King died earlier, before Young Hamlet had been formally recognised as a man, it is likely that the Council would've chosen Lord Claudius as the new King. Now, however, Young Hamlet stood between Lord Claudius and the crown—unless he was murdered as well.

"There's no need to re-hash that," Lord Claudius said. "I chose my way because... well, because war is cleaner than sorcery, and death under the blows of an axe nobler than that brought about by some vile potion. But that is water under the bridge."

He paused for a moment, scratching at his bead. "You have not told me how you plan to administer this poison, how you plan to pour it into the King's ear. He's as closely guarded as any man on God's earth. Not a soul could get near enough."

"Then the poison must be delivered by one who does not possess a soul."

"You, you mean? God's teeth, I knew there was something missing from you, you cold-blooded lizard."

Polonius didn't rise to the insult. "Not I," he said, evenly, "but an agent of mine. Observe."

With this he turned to set a vessel on the brazier and began the chant that I'd heard before. Once more dark and horrible vapours rose sinuously into the air, where they coiled and thickened into the shape I'd tried so hard to forget.

I screamed.

Almost as soon as I'd given myself away, I was leaping down from the rafters, though whether I was seeking to flee from Polonius or from the thing he'd summoned, I don't know. I do know that my clown's technique let me down, however. Instead of falling cleanly and rolling to my feet, I landed on a barrel, lost my balance and went sprawling. I scrabbled for purchase, but already Lord Claudius was blocking the doorway, a dagger in his hand.

It was the mock hunt that saved me. One ploy I sometimes used in my role as the prey was to double back. I'd let myself appear to be cornered, then shoot forward on hands and knees, darting between my master's legs, and the hunt would be on again. Now I was the prey in earnest, and the move my only hope. I lunged towards Lord Claudius, keeping as low to the ground as I could. Fortunately, he was standing with his feet apart, the better (he thought) to block the doorway. I'd scuttled beneath him before he'd realised what I was about, and was soon running as fast as I could back to the main castle.

"Stop him," Claudius shouted. "Polonius, send your creature after him."

If I'd had breath with which to scream again, I would've done so. Visions of being torn limb from limb by that awful creature filled my mind. I ran faster than I've ever run.

———————

Polonius' creature didn't catch me. It probably didn't even chase me. I reached the bottom of the stairs leading up to the chamber I shared with my master and lay there panting. I also frantically tried to cudgel my wits into serving me. I'd spent years appearing half-witted. Had this, as my master had declared, made my wits sharper than most?

First, did Polonius know who'd spied on him? Probably not. One running boy in the dark looks much like another. But he knew that he had been spied upon. Which meant that he'd do what? Flee for his life? Unlikely. No, what he would most probably do was to put his evil scheme into effect straight away, before anyone had time to warn the King.

Which meant I had to act. But how? Who would listen to the ravings of a half-witted clown who disturbed him in the middle of the night?

I flew up the stairs and shook my master. "Wake up!" I cried in his ear. "In the name of the King, wake up!"

"Osric?" he asked, sleepily. "What, have you had a nightmare?"

"A nightmare yes, but a waking one." Rapidly, I told him what I'd seen, and what I thought was about to happen. Too rapidly. He made me slow down and repeat myself. I did so.

Still he did not move. "Hurry, Master, we may have only moments."

"Then we must use them wisely." He was fully awake by now.

"We must warn the King," I urged.

"We must warn someone, but if we burst into the King's chamber one of his guards will strike our heads from our bodies before we've had time to open our mouths."

"Someone of higher status, then."

"Yes, but who? Not Rosencrantz or Guildenstern—they're already in Claudius' pocket. Cornelius, perhaps, or Voltimand? No, I have it: Horatio. He's loyal or no-one is."

A moment later we were racing through the castle in the direction of Horatio's apartments. His servant tried to bar our passage, but he was still half-asleep and my master pushed past him.

The din wakened Lord Horatio so that he was already sitting up in bed and lighting a candle when we approached him. "Yorick," he said in surprise, "and young Osric. Come to amuse me at such a late hour?"

"No, my Lord," my master said, as we bent our knees to him. "We have come because the King's life is threatened, and only you can save it." Briefly, my master related what I'd told him.

Lord Horatio heard my master out. Afterwards he said nothing for a long time. "I think you're knaves or imbeciles," he said at last, "or possibly both. I should have you flogged." I felt sick to my stomach. The King was probably being murdered as we spoke, and Lord Horatio would not act.

"However," Lord Horatio continued, and my heart leapt, "if there's even one chance in a hundred that you are telling me the truth, I am duty bound to act. Boots and my sword," he called to his servant, who scurried to obey. "If, however," Lord Horatio said, turning back to us, "I find that this *is* a wild goose chase, then I will have you flogged without mercy. Now follow."

We were too late. As we approached the King's chamber, we heard the screams. Ghastly, shrill and unearthly they were, such as could scarcely have been made by a human throat. They seemed to last a hideous time, then were suddenly cut off.

There was a heartbeat of terrible silence, then all was confusion—men and women, nobles and servants, some awake and terrified, some drowsy and confused—all made for the King's chamber. My master made as if to join them, but Lord Horatio held him back.

"No, Yorick, there's nothing you can do. You were right, I beg your pardon for my doubts." He thought for a moment. "There's nothing we can do for the King, that is, but we may yet be able to save Young Hamlet. Here —" he thrust his sword into my master's hands, "fetch the Prince and bring him down to Messenger Cove. I have a boat there. A small one, but I can make it ready swiftly. Young Hamlet must be got out of Denmark tonight, or all is lost."

"Where will you go?"

"Where fortune directs. No more words. Go!"

We went. This time we were not too late, though had we paused to blink but once we would have been. I do not know what Polonius' plan for Young

Hamlet had been, but it seemed that I had forced his hand before his preparations were all in place. That is to say that whilst his creature was pouring poison into the ear of the King, Lord Claudius had been forced to take the murder of Young Hamlet into his own hands.

One must allow that he was devilishly cunning, even so. Young Hamlet had his own guards, of course. Though they had been alarmed by the King's screams, they had not abandoned their posts, but dutifully remained in front of the door to Young Hamlet's chamber, their swords in their hands. Lord Claudius approached them, seemingly in a state of great agitation. "Murder!" he cried. "There are assassins in the King's apartments. Go and help apprehend them. I will guard the young lord."

This the guards accepted as true and rushed off. My master and I were in time to see them go; in time to see Lord Claudius draw his sword and enter the chamber of Young Hamlet.

We raced to forestall him. As I burst through the door, I saw the Prince sprawled on the floor. His uncle stood over him, his sword raised as though to administer the death blow. He had his back to me. Almost without thinking, I snatched up a stool and brought it down on Lord Claudius' head. He fell stunned.

Then my master came and stood over him, ready to drive Horatio's sword into the villain's black heart.

"Wait!" It was Young Hamlet who had spoken. "He must not die until he has told all he knows; and even then he must not die quickly."

"No time for that, my King," my master replied.

"King?"

"Aye, King. I own you as such. Your noble father has been murdered, God rest his soul. No time to say more: you must quit Elsinore now, or your reign will be brief indeed. Lord Horatio has a boat ready, or I hope he has."

Thankfully, Young Hamlet had the sense not to argue. He rose to his feet —but when he took a step he gasped in pain. It was then that we saw the blood staining his britches.

"You're hurt," my master said, alarmed.

"A touch I do confess, but not a death-blow."

"Aye, but can you walk?"

Young Hamlet essayed another step. "No," he said.

"Then I must bear you on my back one last time. Come, mount."

Awkwardly, Young Hamlet did so. "Shall I despatch?" my master asked indicating Lord Claudius with the sword he still held.

"No," Young Hamlet said. "My revenge must be delayed, it seems, but I will not be cheated of it. Now, away."

Messenger Cove lies at the foot of the rocks on which Elsinore stands. It is so named because messengers bearing urgent dispatches will often land there, rather than at the main harbour some miles to the south. It is reached by a winding path that is accessed from a postern in the north wall. This we made for, and were relieved to find it unwatched, the guard having presumably been drawn to the commotion elsewhere. I snatched a flaming torch out of its bracket and led the way. I peered anxiously ahead trying to see if a boat was waiting for us. It was too dark to be sure.

As we started down towards the beach, my master called a halt. "He's losing too much blood. You must bind his leg. Here, give me that torch. I'll watch the path."

I ripped my shirt into strips which I wound round Young Hamlet's leg as tightly as possible. They made a crude bandage, but one that would serve, I hoped.

"More than a touch, My Lord," my master observed drily.

"But less than a death-stroke, as I assured you."

My master was about to answer, when I pointed, urgently. There, above us on the path, was Polonius' creature.

Up until now, I have refrained from describing such a blasphemy. I must do so now. It was man-shaped, of small stature and not solid. Instead, it was made up entirely of smoke and vapours. It did not walk down the path, it flowed. That is to say it dissolved itself at one place and re-formed itself at another. I saw then how Polonius had intended to employ it—such a creature could drift through a keyhole or seep under a door, and no guard would be any the wiser.

Torch in one hand, sword in the other, my master turned to face the demon—for so it must've been. It looked on my master. Two eyes, blazing like coals in the hottest part of a blacksmith's forge, shone intensely, as though it was relishing its malice.

"Osric," my master said without turning his head, "carry King Hamlet down to the boat."

"I cannot leave you, Master."

"You must save the King," he said. "Farewell, Osric," he added. "I was right abut you. You will be a great clown. Now go." With that, he braced himself to meet his unearthly foe.

I hoisted Young Hamlet—King Hamlet, I should say—onto my own back, and started towards the beach below. I hadn't gone a dozen steps before I heard my master scream in a most piteous manner. Unnerved, I lost my footing and fell, dropping the King, who hissed with pain.

My nerves failed me. I knew I ought to have helped him up again, but I couldn't move. My eyes were fixed on the demon.

Like a feather in a breeze, it drifted slowly towards me. It carried no weapon that I could see, though I doubted it would need one. The King seemed to have swooned. I dragged him behind a large rock, though what use I thought hiding might be I could not have said.

The demon approached and loomed over me, seeming to grow in stature as it did so. Not knowing what else to do, I lay on top of the King, trying to shield him with my body. Clown tricks, I thought, would not serve me here time.

Petrified, I waited for the demon to strike. I waited for what seemed an age but the demon did nothing. Then, incredibly, it dissipated into the darkness.

I did not have time to thank the Saints for my deliverance, nor to wonder at its cause. Peering round the rock, I saw that there were figures above me, coming down the path. Polonius was there, and his sinister servant, Reynaldo, bearing a torch. Lords Rosencrantz and Guildenstern were close behind, swords in their hands.

My heart sank. Polonius had recalled his demon because it was no longer needed. Swords can kill as easily. Then I saw a fifth person above me. Queen Gertrude. She pushed her way past the men and barred Polonius' path. She spoke rapidly. I did not hear her words, but it was plain that she was in a great fury.

In a flash I saw all. Whether my wits had truly been sharpened by my master's training, or whether some blessed power looked kindly on me, I do not know, but I saw all. Queen Gertrude was privy to the plot, that was plain. Or, at the least, she was privy to the plot to murder the Old King, and place her lover on the throne in his stead. But she was *not* privy to the plot to murder Young Hamlet, her son. What mother could countenance such a thing?

Was his mother's love enough to save Young Hamlet? It seemed little enough on which to stake his life. Claudius might be swayed by his love for Queen Gertrude, but Polonius would surely see him as a threat.

But how if he was not a threat?

I shook the King, urgently. "Awake," I hissed into his ear.

"What?" he asked groggily. I shook him again, but could get little sense out of him.

I saw that desperate measures were called for. I clamped one hand over his mouth, whilst with the other I jabbed at his wound.

The pain jerked him awake.

"I am sorry, my King," I told him, "but we have only moments. You have lost your wits." I took my hand off his mouth.

"I have?"

"It must seem so. There is no time to tell all, but if you are to live, you must pose no threat to any. A man without wits is no threat."

Young Hamlet considered this. "I must be mad?"

"It must seem so, for a little while at least."

"Then I shall be mad north-north-west. When the wind turns southerly again, I shall know what I shall know."

Above us on the path, Polonius and his fellows were perilously near. "God bless you, my King," I said, and scuttled crabwise into the darkness.

The last thing I heard was Young Hamlet's voice as Polonius looked down on him. "I know you, sirrah," he said. "I think you are a fishmonger."

Afterwards, I crept back to where the body of my master lay. There was no mark on him to show how he had died. I believe the demon simply sucked the life out of him.

Alas, Poor Yorick

I took him in my arms and bore him away.

The Council met the next day, and proclaimed Lord Claudius King. King Hamlet, they declared, had been murdered by enemies of Denmark, who had also attempted to carry off Young Hamlet. Though they had been unsuccessful in the second part of their plan, Young Hamlet's wits had been disturbed as a result. How many of the Council believed this tale, and how many had been part of the plot all along, I don't know. Claudius was acknowledged as King, I say, though Polonius stood close behind his throne. Which of the two held the other in thrall I neither knew nor cared.

Young Hamlet continues to play his part. He speaks little and laughs less, spending most of his days withdrawn in his own private chamber. Every so often, however, he catches my eye in a knowing manner. There's method in his madness, I deem, and vengeance in his heart. When the time is ripe, he will reclaim his birthright. Whether Claudius and Polonius realise this, and whether they still desire his death, I cannot say—but for the nonce Queen Gertrude holds them in check.

As soon as was seemly (too soon in many eyes), King Claudius married Queen Gertrude. There was much carousing at the wedding feast, and much clowning. Oh yes, I assumed my master's role. What else could I have done? I know no other trade. My life, I know, will be forfeit if Claudius or Polonius realise how much I know, but neither of them ever had a clear sight of me on that terrible night—and who would ever suspect a clown of being anything other than a half-wit?

At the wedding feast, I capered, jested and set the table on a roar. Polonius did not laugh.

Afterwards I went and shed tears on a grave I'd dug with my own hands.

Alas, my poor master. Alas, the man who was the nearest I'd ever had to a father.

Alas, poor Yorick.

———————

G.K. Lomax is a nom-de-internet. Behind it lies a rather strange individual from the fair English county of Essex. His stories can be found in a number of anthologies, most recently *1816: the Year without a Summer* and *Discordant Love Beyond Death*. He is currently working on the memoirs of Bartie Lovecraft—stories of cosmic horror in the style of P G Wodehouse.

He has appeared on four broadcast quiz shows, has been cursed by Sean Connery for the errant nature of his golf, and sometimes thinks the end of the world can't come soon enough.

Follow him on Twitter: @GKLomax343 and @BartieLovecraft

Please consider leaving an honest review

Reviews are vital for readers and authors. Every review that readers leave helps hundreds of other people find new books to love. And it can make or break a book.

So, if you enjoyed this book, please write an honest review on the site where you found it. Reviews mean more readers, and more readers mean that I can publish more books featuring great stories by talented authors.

Looking for more clowning?

Bloody Red Nose:

Fifteen Fears of a Clown

In a world filled with menace, dare to paint on a grin.

The world is full of images of scary clowns: packs of grinning figures with knives plaguing towns; pom-pom clad serial killers; loners who like children in the wrong way.

But clowns can be a force for good: it takes a kind heart to put other people's joy first; keeping children entertained is honest work; what better disguise than one that makes the villains laugh?

What if, rather than being childhood-spoiling serial killers, clowns were the victims or heroes of the story?

When all the children at a party are poisoned, an entertainer's profession and past both make him a prime suspect.

An anti-corporate prankster discovers his guru might be just as callous as the capitalist world-view he claims to reject.

A clown attempts to redeem the image of his profession by saving a group of teenagers from a serial killer.

And twelve more stories of clowns facing humanity's baser natures.

Find it at your favourite retailer today.
ISBN (Paperback): 978-1-912674-09-1
ISBN (EPUB): 978-1-912674-10-7
ISBN (MOBI): 978-1-912674-11-4

Made in the USA
Las Vegas, NV
28 February 2021